ALVARADO

ALVARADO

John W. Horton III

atmosphere press

PROLOGUE
The Blue Light

I

She said that she would put a blue light on at night and that it would mean that she was working. I thought about that for a while. About what it really meant. I wasn't much of a hustler, though I wanted to be a writer and that was something that drove me to the outer limits. Angela was a cold capitalist, athlete and friend. She had dirty money. She was a hustler. Her adolescence was spent in Germany because her father was in the military. She was originally from St. Louis.

Somehow we had crossed paths. She knew how to make things happen. I had known a lot of different types of people and she was unique. She had a way with people. She had guts and, well, she was a talented painter, a bass player and an athlete. I caved—in the end because I couldn't go through with it all. The things she wanted me to do and had tried to encourage me to do. I thought I could live so many ways, but I found that I had reached a wall. It wasn't that I didn't care though; I later found myself wandering through the streets of west Los Angeles mostly on the public bus. It was the hustler in her. We all had our dark sides and I had mine. I knew she had been through a lot and had run down the whole story to me about her family and brother being addicted to crack and her other brother who was selling it to him just to keep him off the streets. The other brother who had done well and was looked up to in the neighborhood. All that and tickets around the world. How far could the world really go and how many times could we swing ourselves around it until we were just too dizzy to stand up? I thought about her and that blue light that she left on and the taste of sugar, how it all made me feel. When I could be saying so much about life and I somehow couldn't find the words to say anything at all about her. She was beautiful in her own kind of way but I wasn't attracted to her in the way that she might have felt about me, and I think that's why it all ended the way that it did. I didn't see in her what the men who patronized her did. She was more than a prostitute; she was my friend and a human being.

I had met her in school. We both lived off campus. In the afternoon we would take off into the city. Later I learned that she had a picture and a name in the back of the alternative press newspaper where I was interning. One day, while working in the advertising department, she came into lobby to place an advertisement, and that's when I learned the truth.

"Do you know I'm sleeping with one of the editors at your paper?" she asked me. It was hot that day. We were standing on the sidewalk on Sunset Boulevard. She wore sunglasses and we were face-to-face.

I didn't know what to say.

She had a book that had been written by one of the

editors who solicited her for hand-jobs, sex and maybe more. He had autographed it.

She gave it to me.

"Look here in your paper," she told me.

I reached down to a copy of the paper that was in her apartment and there inside the cover was the name of one of my editors. I stood there for a long time looking at the name. There was a gulf of silence that I felt. That everything was fake. What had I gotten myself into now?

I dropped the paper on the small coffee table. She looked at me and lit a cigarette.

"You wanna smoke some weed?"

I nodded my head. She came over and hugged me and kissed me. I took the book and threw it against the wall. I wanted to throw it through the window but I stopped at the last minute. She backed away from me and finished her cigarette, nervously walking into the kitchen. Now the paper looked so small. I stared at the book lying on the floor. I worked diligently but now that I knew so much, I started to feel detached. I took two buses to get to work and now I was high most of the time because it was so early in the morning and I started to smoke more and more marijuana as I walked up Highland. I always passed a bookstore where I sometimes stole books to read at work. My hair began to grow long. I was lonely and started seeing a girl at work. Here I was trying my best to play it straight, to see things a certain way, and now I knew that things were way beyond my understanding, that somehow I once again had shown myself to be so naive. I knew about what she was doing before and how she had acquired the BMW in a student loan scam with a man who had also been a patron. She also had a motorcycle. The manager of our share-house spied on her one time, looking through the window of her room and we caught him and I told him off. What really blew everything up was that different men kept coming to that place to see her. People started getting suspicious of what she was doing. I knew all along, but everybody else couldn't put it all together; however, they suspected it later and my editor, a middle-aged white woman who liked black men from the Caribbean, asked me about her and I said I didn't know what he was talking about.

She knew that I thought a lot about race and how it had affected my whole life. She questioned my writing but she knew that a lot of people were reading what I was writing and that a lot of the African American students on campus read what I was writing. She liked me but eventually I was fired from my college paper. Though one of my editorials was submitted by the same editor and had won an award. Amanda kissed me on the cheek after the English Department Chair gave me my prestigious award. I felt triumphant in a way, even though I felt like I was falling at the same time. Amanda pressed her breasts against me. Our editor, a middle-aged white woman, had been in a few bands, had two master's degrees and she liked black men but I wasn't attracted to her. I didn't want to fuck her.

Amanda was Armenian, from Russia. I had photographed her on campus. One job at the paper was to go out and question students on certain issues. That's how I found her. I had given her one of my fictional stories. We talked a lot on the phone. In one particular column I had written about how I had cut school and went to downtown Oakland to see a Russian foreign film that featured a

Russian Playboy Playmate. I must have been the youngest person in the audience. When I should have been at school, I was downtown at the Oakland public library checking out books and listening to records. She came to the school newspaper the next day because she wanted a story to be written about the Armenian Genocide in 1914. I did. I met her in the hallway outside the paper. She was wearing a white dress that seemed a little revealing but it was traditional in some way. We hugged and she kissed me and she thanked me. Somehow I felt I represented a distinct journalist generation at school that had taken things to where previous generations had not. So now life had become a little less mysterious and more competitive. It all got me down sometimes because I had gotten fired. But some arrangement was worked out for me to still write stories. I still felt destitute. Amanda drifted away from me and toward her Russian-Armenian crowd. I danced with her for the last time at her birthday party in Glendale.

Writing seemed the only way out. I ended up at an alternative newspaper in Hollywood. Maybe it was getting fired that set me on this path and following all of my passions for a few months, taking magic mushrooms with a friend and driving across the city hallucinating; we had become daring. Things had become so distorted but we did not interfere with destiny. I saw clearly and the next day aced a math test for the only class I had left to get my BA. It was addicting. I wanted more trips because I wanted to forget about it all. I missed Amanda but I lusted for Iko.

After college and interning by day, I delved into Persian cinema, shown late at night on Second Street, in Santa Monica. I was killing time. I smoked a joint on the way to the cinema and then would pay for a ticket and then sit in the back row. Sometimes mushrooms made it to heavy. I took my time on La Cienega Boulevard. waiting for Angela to stop turning tricks. I was always stoned and going for long walks. I was looking for food. The prostitutes were outside the cheap motels. It looked different without all the cars. Things had been completely turned upside down. Everything that I thought could be reality had become surreal. The editor at the alternative press where I was barely making a living was giving me the blues. My boss whom I had become so excited to know had become my worst enemy. We didn't like each other anymore. She stopped leaving her blouse a little open like she used to when I would walk into her office. I didn't want to fuck her either. All of this aggressiveness had driven me mad. I wanted to be a famous writer so bad.

What did I want?

What did she want?

There was something else I was after. It wasn't the voluptuous black female staff writer who was dating some white guy, who had given me some advice. But not only that, I admired her for her intelligence and writing abilities. I wanted to be as successful as her. I had put so much pressure on myself. I took to the streets in my own sort of fucked up way. I had to make sense of it all. I had to put all the dots together and all that other shit. Now I felt some sort of freedom. Somehow I had gone over the edge and had drifted toward some unknown world. What had happened? I wasn't sure. My greatest love had become my greatest burden. It was leading me into the ground. I had this lust that I had to satisfy.

I had met a voluptuous female Vietnamese writer the night before. She was inspiring and ambitious; she'd graduated from UCLA. I was at a bar in Chinatown, talking to another writer actually, and was invited by an older Japanese man, a comedian, who owned some lofts in the Arts District near Little Tokyo. He was some sort of celebrity and looked like Don Ho. He liked to drink and entertain and it was there at Taix Restaurant that I had met him and the female Vietnamese writer for the first time. Somehow we ended up talking and she gave me a ride home while listening to hip-hop but that was before all this other stuff happened.

I had really come to Taix because I was following a lead. The older Japanese gentlemen Mr. Sakamoto that I somehow met at Taix on Sunset weeks earlier was doing comedy with another man. It was low budget. It was cool. It was sort of a milder version of Jerry Louis and Dean Martin. He seemed to know everyone. Later he sort of ran down the whole beginnings of the West Coast computer industry and I was running out of tape on my tape recorder and the day before I had met another writer in my building and she said that I should read the *Virgin Suicides* and write like its author Eugenides. She had some heroin and she asked if I wanted any and I had never tried it before and so she lit it in a cigarette and I smoked it and when it was time to leave I floated back to my room and lay in the bed. She came by the next day to ask how I was doing and she wasn't wearing a bra and she had really large breasts.

II

Kendra and Pauline lived on the third floor that overlooked our street. I thought back. The building with the trees in front.

"That was a cool place but getting the dog, that was a bad idea," I said to myself. "That sort of marked the end."

Iko liked that apartment. I had seen Pauline twice. That was the climax of the relationship. Pauline had seen Iko one time in passing. Before I would really get to know Pauline, I noticed something about her eyes. They seemed so serious but livid at the same time. Here is where the writing and fantasy collided into some sort of vortex. I put my hands on my forehead.

Kendra was from New Jersey. She seemed quite wealthy but ambivalent about life. Her relationship with Kendra was unorthodox. Her father owned a chain of porno theaters across New Jersey. She was in school at one time but now it didn't seem to matter.

"Give the blunt to Kendra Bernal," said Pauline smiling.

I passed her the blunt.

"She used to roll blunts and hang with black guys," said Pauline.

"Will you shut up, Pauline!" said Kendra. "And all you did was suck dick!" Pauline said lastly to end the conversation.

Kendra turned on her side. Her face was red. She had been embarrassed where before she felt so much in control, Pauline was always airing Kendra's dirty laundry.

I sat quietly. I stared straight ahead. I wondered how two women could live together, knowing that women could be so cold, colder than men.

Pauline jumped down from the top bunk bed and left

Kendra brooding. She was nude and so casual about what she was doing, it was as if she had clothes on. I stared ahead but watched her as she approached the open window. She was so sensual. She smiled. I watched her as she slowly approached the window, slightly bending over, looking outside, then pulling herself back in and shutting the window. Kendra was watching too. Pauline stood at the window for a moment, long enough to show me everything she had to offer. I was motionless.

"Why don't you just say you want to fuck him?" Kendra blurted out sarcastically.

Pauline looked toward Kendra. She took her time. She was tempting and still smiling. She glanced a little toward me and walked back to the top bunk and climbed back in bed with Kendra. She had a grin as I sat across the room with my back toward the door. Now I felt on edge. She came up with another blunt nicely rolled that she had stashed away and came back down from the bunk again. She handed it to me and then turned and walked away and sat down on a chair with her knees pulled up to her chest spread wide. She produced a lighter and handed it to me. I stood up as she lit the blunt and I took a few puffs before passing it to Kendra. Somehow the other blunt had just disappeared.

"Nice blunt," she said.

Pauline started laughing. Kendra passed her the blunt and she took a few more puffs before passing it back to me. By this time we were all high. Pauline sat in a chair opposite me and with her knees still bent toward her chest and legs open.

Kendra would never really talk about her life but at the same time she had some type of angst in her. Almost as if she was unhappy. Then her relationship with Pauline seemed like another fantasy and I wondered about the erotic nature and flirtatiousness of Pauline and the coy nature of Kendra. As much as I might feel repulsed by them, I somehow was drawn to them. Kendra gave me a look of pity, as if to say she felt sorry for me.

"Was that your girlfriend I saw that day?" asked Pauline.

"Who?" I asked with my head in my hands.

"The Japanese girl?"

"Yeah."

"She's beautiful!"

I looked up. I was trying to block Iko out of my mind. She had only left a week ago.

"Are you okay?" asked Pauline, with her legs wide open.

"Yeah I'm okay and thanks. I just miss her a lot," I said trying not to look up.

"I don't know where we are going but I love her a lot but I know she won't be around for long; I just don't want to face the facts."

"Don't worry about it," said Kendra trying to be reassuring.

I kept my hands to my head covering my eyes.

"Does she give good head?" asked Pauline laughing.

"Will you shut up," said Kendra annoyed. "Can't you see he's depressed."

"I heard you guys fucking when she was here. She wanted to stop but you wanted to keep going. It must be too big! Everyone could hear, you know, I mean these walls are so fucking thin!"

I looked up and stared at Pauline. She stopped smiling.

I opened the front door of their apartment and closed it behind me and exited.

I could hear Kendra telling Pauline she was fucked up. I could hear Pauline's loud laughing as I walked down the hallway and back toward my apartment. I opened the door to my apartment. It was dark. I closed the door and lay down on the bed facedown. I was still very high and I closed my eyes. Pauline's wicked laugh echoed in my head.

III

The next day I heard a knock at the door. I got up and walked over to it. I looked through the peep hole and saw that it was Pauline. Hesitating, I opened the door.

"What do you want?" I asked.

"I came to say I'm sorry," she said, tilting her head a little bit to the side.

"Thank you," I said and slammed the door in her face and walked away.

"Can I come in? I want to talk to you!" she said shouting from the other side of the door.

I stopped and looked at the floor and then turned around and went to the door and opened it a little bit.

"I'm really sorry, can I come in?" she asked again.

I looked at her and then opened the door and walked over to my bed and sat down again. Pauline had her little dog, a miniature Doberman Pincher.

"Nice dog," I said watching the dog sniff around my apartment.

"I'm going to walk my dog. Do you want to come with

me?" she asked me. She had on bright red lipstick, a green shirt, a yellow skirt with tights underneath and a green German military winter army coat, with fur around the hood. She sat down next to me and put her hand on my leg.

"Don't do that," I said to her.

"Don't do what?" said Pauline looking straight ahead out a large window that was covered by a yellow sheet.

"I like you," she said.

"I thought you were gay?" I said a little confused.

She moved her hand closer toward my crotch.

"You're fucking crazy. I don't like you that way," I said a little nervously, grabbing her hand.

"You're so naive!" she said putting her hand on the zipper to my pants.

I put my hand on her hand and pulled it away.

"What's wrong, I'm not good enough for you?" she asked looking me in the eye.

"Why can't you look at me? You don't fuck white girls!" she said glaring. I could see her perfect rows of white clinched teeth.

I looked up at her. She smiled, stood up, and took off her jacket and sat down again.

"I like guys too, okay, it's just that... well, I don't trust men that much. When I was younger my cousin tried to rape me. I guess that's when I just didn't care anymore."

"You're the second girl that has told me that," I said wondering what the hell I was getting into.

"I'm Egyptian and Greek and I came here from Toronto."

"You want an award!" I said sarcastically. Pauline still had her hand between my legs.

She smiled.

"Where's Kendra?" I asked.

"She's at her mother's house. Stand up!" she said.

"What?" I said gulping.

Pauline slapped me.

"Are you fucking crazy?" I said standing up. "Get the fuck out of here, you crazy bitch!"

"No! I'm sorry!" she said apologetically.

"What the fuck do you want from me?" I screamed.

Pauline stood up and pulled me toward her and started kissing me, slowly moving her hands down my sides.

"Fuck me, okay! Just fuck me! Don't you know when a girl wants to fuck? No wonder she left you! I'm sorry ...shit!"

I took my hands and placed them under her skirt and pulled her tights and panties down and we both fell back on my bed.

"I have a condom, don't worry," said Pauline, pulling it out of her coat pocket. Then she slowly removed her underwear, tights and shoes, throwing them on the floor next to her coat.

Pauline handed the condom to me. She watched me try to put it on. She stopped me. Her dog sat down on a chair on the other side of the room.

"Can I touch it?" asked Pauline.

"What?" I asked confused at what was happening.

She grabbed my penis and held it in her hands and looked at it for a while.

"It's beautiful!"

She then opened her mouth bent down over my lap and put my penis in her mouth and started bobbing her head up and down like a wild machine.

She stopped after I came. She wiped her mouth with her hand. Her lipstick was smeared across her cheek and her right wrist. She spit my semen in a garbage can near the bed.

"Shit!" she said and started laughing again, with cum on the corner of her mouth.

"Ahhh, my mouth hurts, that was torture ...just put the condom on."

I tried to put the condom on quickly, but it was hard to do.

"You're so lame. You have to dry it off first," said Pauline. She put the condom on one of my sheets and wiped off my penis and then put the condom on it. She then lay back on the bed and stuck her legs in the air. One of them hit the wall, making a loud sound and she laughed.

"Come on I can't wait all day. I have to walk my dog later," she said jokingly.

I lay on top of her.

"Wow, you learn fast! Come on!"

I started moving up and down. Pauline tilted her head back more and pressed me against her.

"That's it, don't be afraid! You're so good... come on push harder," she said smiling wrapping her legs around my back.

I kept moving.

"Bend me over and fuck me . . . come on . . . come on!" she yelled urging me to turn her around.

I turned her over and pulled her skirt back toward her shoulders and entered her.

"Oh my god... that hurts like hell!" she said trying to stop me.

"Damn! I can't do this anymore!"

I kept going.

"Stop!" she yelled, tilting her head to the side, her teeth biting her lips.

I wouldn't stop. Pauline put her head in the pillow and lay her head down and then she went limp after several minutes. I pulled away from her and sat back on my bed.

"Kendra can't do that!" she said breathing heavily.

"Are you happy now?" I asked sitting on the edge of the bed, sweating.

She slapped me again, laughing.

"What was that for?" I asked dumbfounded, wanting to hit her back.

"Don't be sad, didn't you know what you were getting into? You want to go for a walk with me? I think we need some fresh air," she said looking up at the ceiling.

"Do you have any weed? I need to smoke."

I rolled a joint and lit it, took a few puffs and then handed it to Pauline. She took a puff handed it back to me and put on her underwear.

"Lay down next to me," she said making room for me to lie down next to her.

"You're so strange," she said puffing on the joint again before handing it to me again.

"You're so quiet and I think girls would like you more if you would just open up more."

"Girls always approach me like you," I said wondering why had opened my apartment door.

"Yeah, because you don't get it! I mean damn, and well, also you don't have any money either!"

"So that's all that matters?" I asked handing her the joint back.

"Women need security. You know how I got here. I met

some rich old fucker. He lived in Santa Monica. I left home and well I went to live with him, but he was a total pervert. I just left him and then I met Kendra. She's rich, you know, and well, here I am. I really want to marry someone so I can stay here but everyone I meet turns out to be some creep!" she said tapping me on the shoulder to pass me the joint.

"How can you meet anyone decent when you're so fucking perverted yourself?"

Pauline stopped and lay her head back on her hand.

"Don't you want to know any more about my life?" she asked me.

"Let's go for a walk," I said

Pauline sat up and looked at me.

"She doesn't want to be with you because you're not successful as a writer. I know that now," said Pauline. "But she keeps you around because well, you never know. That's how women are!"

"Let's go for a walk!" I said."

"You think I don't know that?" I asked looking at Pauline. "Fix your lipstick!" I yelled at her in frustration.

Pauline looked at me and smiled.

We both put our clothes on. Pauline went to my bathroom and washed her face and put her lipstick back on. Her hair was short and dark black. She was cool and confident. Nothing seemed to phase her, as if she could handle herself in a war. She wasn't intimidated easily. I went in after her and washed my face and put on a fresh shirt and a sweater and grabbed my jacket and we left my apartment.

"Our neighborhood sucks!" said Pauline smiling again. Always that strange smile on her face. Her dog led the way.

"My parents are Greek immigrants that came to Toronto. My dad owned a restaurant. He made a lot of money. We have a large house with a pool. I liked this Jamaican guy when I was in high school. My parents were against it. My father is racist."

"That's why you fuck black guys, to get back at your father?" I said sarcastically.

Pauline stopped and looked at me.

"I didn't know you had a sense of humor!" she said and kept walking down the street. She pulled out a cigarette and lit it and then pulled some sunglasses out of the pocket of her jacket and put them on. They were very dark, black and plastic, but they looked expensive.

"You know that show *Degrassi Junior High*?" she asked me.

"Yeah, I know that show," I said laughing.

Pauline started to laugh too.

"Well I auditioned for that show and I was rejected. They said I was too pretty."

"What?" I said in amazement.

"What? What? That's all you say, you're so stupid," Pauline said laughing.

"Yeah, they said I was too pretty and that they needed someone with a different look. Remember in the show there was this black guy who was dating this white girl?"

"Yeah!"

"Well that was supposed to be me because she was Greek too."

"I can't believe this," I said bewildered.

"Well, believe it. It's true. I really wanted that role. I was already modeling but I kept doing it but I wasn't happy at home though. I mean I was supposed to be this nice Greek girl and I was fucking this Jamaican guy, my dad and I argued all the time. It's funny because it was really happening to me and I was auditioning for this part for a television show where it was fictional."

"Art imitating life!"

"Crazy shit, right?!" Pauline said.

I looked up at the sky. The sky was bright blue. The sun kept us warm even though winter was approaching. Central American immigrants were milling about on a street. They passed a bakery. The streets were crowded and dirty. As they headed farther west the scenery began to change.

"How about you?" asked Pauline.

"What about me?" I asked.

"I mean what are you? You're not totally black."

"My mother is French-Creole."

"So can you speak French?" asked Pauline.

"No. My mother's parents spoke it, but she never learned it."

"I can speak French but that's only because I grew up in Canada."

"My mother's parents left New Orleans and when they came to California, they were passing for white—pas en blanc!"

"That's so crazy."

"Your father is black?"

"Yeah, he's really dark."

"Did you have a hard time growing up?" asked Pauline looking over at me.

"You know what's it like being one of only two black kids in a school and whenever a black girl comes around everyone tells you she's for you. That you should go and talk to her as if they know what is best for you."

"You don't like black women."

"I like black women, but they don't like me."

"You don't act black."

"What?" I said. "I guess white girls don't seem to mind it when it comes to sex!"

"I'm not a white girl!" She replied smiling. "You're so complex. I don't want to be like this, but I just wanted to fuck you. I like fucking black guys."

"What do you really want, Pauline? You are so confusing. Maybe I am too but you're dating a girl. You come to my apartment and give me a blowjob and then you want me to fuck you as hard as I can. What am I getting myself into? I'm lonely too. I mean ... why should I turn you down. You're crazy but you're beautiful. I would marry you to help you stay in America, but you're right— I'm a poor writer living in Los Angeles with a Japanese girlfriend whose parents are yuppies."

"I like black guys, but I can't marry anyone who is black."

"Does that make any fucking sense? What you really want is a normal life, but you are not normal. You want it all and you always get what you want!" I said taking off her sunglasses and looking her in the eyes.

Pauline smiled and took her sunglasses out of my hands and put them back on her face and smiled. "Yeah, I'm spoiled. I want a rich guy with a big dick, but I can't seem to find one. I want to be loved but I don't trust men but I need affection so I get it from women."

"Are you going to go home someday?" I asked.

"Yeah I'll go home because I can't do this forever and we can't fuck anymore."

"You're right. I'm naive because I let all these women use me, but I want to be loved too. I want something real, but I don't know what is real. Everything comes from the color black, but nothing can come from the color white. I'm just your fantasy."

"I wanted to have sex with you the first time I saw you." Pauline said honestly.

"All you girls are the same!"

"Everyone likes what they can't have," Pauline admitted, taking a few last puffs from her cigarette before smashing it beneath her shoes on the ground.

"How far is this park?" I asked.

"We're almost there."

They continued to walk and then after three blocks they reached the park. There were children playing and birds singing. Pauline motioned for them to sit down on a bench.

"I really enjoy talking to you. I had fun today. Don't tell Kendra about what happened, I can't afford to lose her now."

"Sure! I'll just tell her you gave me a Gyro."

Pauline put her hand on my face and turned my face toward hers and pressed her lips against mine. It seemed like an hour had gone by.

"What was that for?" I asked.

"You are a strange one ...that's what I like about you. You just seem so aloof."

Pauline took out another cigarette and lit it, inhaling.

"I don't want to go home. I just want to sit here forever. Did you enjoy it?"

"Enjoy what?" I asked.

"Did you enjoy having sex with me?"

"I don't know. I never made love like that before. I don't even know you," I said.

Pauline laughed.

"I've been all over the world. When I was younger my mother took me on a train ride across Europe and then we went across the Middle East. It was dangerous, especially when we got to the Middle East, because of the men; ah, they were awful. I liked Morocco the best. My uncle is from Morocco."

"Sounds like you had a good time."

"It was fun. I miss those days."

"Now you're here in fucked up Los Angeles."

"Have you ever been to New York?" Pauline asked me.

"No!"

"You should go, I think it would be better for you. I mean you're a writer."

"That' what everyone keeps telling me."

"Can I read some of your fictional stories?" Pauline asked.

"You know I work at the newspaper."

"Yeah, I know. I've seen one of your articles. I didn't read any of them though. I just looked at them for a long time."

"Why didn't you read them?"

"I don't know."

"You don't care!"

"I care. Who's that black girl with the BMW?"

"A friend," I said mysteriously.

"Are you fucking her?"

"She's gay."

"You like gay girls?"

"We went to college together. She was a fan of my

writing. Now she's a prostitute," I said revealing too much.

"Are you serious?"

"She's fucking one of my editors at the paper. I don't really like the guy but she told me about it last week. She has an advertisement in the back of the paper. She gave me an autographed copy of a book written by the guy who's paying for her services. He turned down one of my story ideas."

"I can't believe this. So, this is why you don't care about anything," Pauline said, lighting another cigarette. "Your life is crazy."

"It's fucking normal!" I said.

Pauline laughed.

"Now I know why you are so disconnected. Your life is full of disappointments."

"I want to quit but I need the money."

"Don't quit. You should write about all of this," said Pauline, inhaling deeply and blowing smoke out of her nose.

"Nobody will care. I'm nobody."

"You are so cold but you're hot when you're with me," she said smiling at me.

"Sounds like a song."

Pauline laughed again.

"What's her name?"

"Angela."

"What's her real name?" Pauline asked again.

"Angela."

"She must make a lot of money."

"Not really."

"Did you fuck her?" asked Pauline.

"No."

"Why not?"

"I'm not attracted to her."

"You're attracted to me?"

"Yes."

"You're so strange."

"So are you."

"Let's get some coffee."

"Okay!"

"You have so many secrets," she said looking me in the eye.

"I'm not the only one."

We left the park and began to walk toward another street.

"Have you ever been on this street before?" asked Pauline.

"No, I just drive past it."

"There's a coffee house over there."

"Looks sort of ritzy"

"Yeah people here have money."

"Do you come here a lot?"

"Sometimes with Kendra but not too often."

They found a coffee shop with a table outside because Pauline was with her dog.

"What do you want?" asked Pauline.

"I want an expresso."

"You need a latte."

"I thought ..."

"Trust me," Pauline said, interrupting me and and walked away to get our coffees.

"Okay!"

"I'll be back."

I sat down at a table and Pauline's dog settled down

under the table but growled when another dog walked by. Pauline returned with our drinks. Two girls at another table noticed her sitting down and stared at us and then turned away.

"What's all that about?"

"They're from the Middle East."

"How do you know?"

"I've been here before, and well, look at me a little more carefully."

I stopped for a moment and looked at her.

"Yeah, I think I know what you mean."

"See, looks can be deceiving, as you Americans like to say."

"If only they knew who you really were."

"They couldn't handle it."

I smiled and took a sip of my Latte.

"You need to write more. You have so much to say even though you look like you don't care about anything."

"I'm trying to."

"I can't believe we are here. Today has been so wild but Kendra was right. I wanted to ... and well I couldn't resist. I didn't think you were going to let me into your apartment."

"I didn't really want to but I felt like you wanted to say you were sorry. The rest was really unexpected!"

One of the girls that was looking at them earlier approached their table.

"Can I get a light from you?" she asked Pauline.

"Sure."

She bent down, showing a little too much cleavage.

"Where are you from?" the girl asked, and then inhaled from the cigarette.

"I'm from Canada."

"Are you Arabic?"

"My mother is from Egypt."

"I'm Syrian. Thank you for the light."

"No problem."

The lady smiled and turned away toward her friend, starting up a conversation in Arabic.

"She's beautiful."

"She would never talk to you, Bernal," says Pauline as she watched the woman talk away with her friend.

"You're so sure about that."

"Kiss me then."

I kissed her on the lips. The Syrian women looked over at us. Pauline smiled as our lips pressed together.

"Are they watching us?"

I tried to discretely look in their direction.

"Yes!" I say as my lips pressed against Pauline's. She smiled and pulled away from me, then kissed me again.

IV

"You know I'm quitting the paper?"

"Really!"

"You think I can work there after all that shit you told me about you fucking one of the editors? And also I'm going nowhere."

"What are you going to do?" Angela asked.

"I don't know."

I sat for a moment in Angela's car. There was a long period of silence. She looked out the window and up at an open window on the fourth floor of my building. There was girl in the window smoking a cigarette looking down at her car.

"Do you know that girl?"

"Yeah."

"She's a white girl?"

"Not exactly."

"What does that mean?"

"Well, she's mixed like Greek and Egyptian or something."

"Did you fuck her?"

I was quiet.

"Well?" asked Angela lifting her eyeglasses above her head for a moment and looking over at me.

"She fucked me."

"So it was like that?" asked Angela

"I guess so . . . let's go."

Angela looked out the window and up again at the window where Pauline was staring down at them but Pauline was gone.

"She's gay."

"Oh really," said Angela, smiling.

"Yeah."

"But that doesn't matter to you?"

"I didn't really want to fuck her, but she just came over to my apartment and she started coming on to me, gave me a blowjob and then we just did ...fucked."

"You're a lucky guy."

"The strange thing about it was I didn't really enjoy it. I mean it was so weird. She's extreme! Wild, diabolical! Shit! Do you have any weed?" I asked, putting on my sunglasses.

"Do you want to go to my apartment?"

"Yeah. . . let's go."

"You sound down for a guy who just got laid. Don't tell me ... wait, Iko?" asked Angela sarcastically.

"You should forget about her. If she really cared about you, she would be here. I think you would be better off with that chick up there in the window."

"She's already taken."

"I think you need something new like a new girl or something. You have to let go. I mean I hate to tell you this but Iko is probably fucking someone else, if what you are saying is true and you just fucked some girl yesterday! I mean you looked so depressed when you came back from Japan," Angela said, trying to find some weed in her pocket.

"Everything just seems so fucked up right now. I was so excited when I started out at the paper. I was so stupid. Then I had a fight with my boss and then I started screwing these other girls and now I'm like about to walk away from it all. College was so much easier, now I'm just another guy who wants to be famous."

"I like your writing," Angela said smiling, trying to cheer me up. She kissed me on the cheek.

"Maybe you should get a hustle like me."

"Like what?"

"Well you could sell weed or something."

"No way!" I said, leaning back in the passenger chair.

"Well, I was going to ask you if you wanted to move out and live with me because I sort of need your help."

"Yeah."

"Well I need to move because my neighbors are getting nosy about what I'm doing and it's making things complicated for me."

"Where are you moving too?"

"I want to move to the West Side, maybe Palms or something."

"Yeah."

"What do you need me for?" I asked.

"Well if you move into my place it will look like I have a normal relationship and my neighbors won't get suspicious, besides I kind of want someone there while I'm doing my thing because it gets kind of crazy sometimes and well I might need your help."

"Sounds heavy."

"Well I'll give you some time to think about it. I mean I know you just moved here and you're getting some action here, but those chicks aren't going to stick around, and you don't have much money either. Believe me I know."

"You know me so well."

"I'm a woman. You want something to drink."

"Like some beer?" I asked looking out the window.

"Yeah a fucking forty ounce or something."

"Okay."

Angela drives north on Vermont until she reaches a liquor store.

"You need to cheer up. I hate seeing you like this. You're starting to make me feel depressed."

"I'm okay. I just have a lot on my mind."

"Hey ... forget about that Japanese bitch. I mean what's important is what is happening right now!" she said ferociously.

I stared out the window as we pull up to a liquor store. Angela gets out of the car and puts out her cigarette.

We return to her apartment.

"Do you ever think about getting a regular job?"

"I can't do that. I'm making too much money and I'm having too much fun."

"Are you happy?"

"No."

"Maybe I need to get out of Los Angeles."

"Maybe you need to hang out a little bit more and meet some different people," said Angela smiling.

"I don't know."

"Didn't you meet some new girl at the paper?"

"Yeah."

"What happened with her?"

"She quit the paper too, but she has a master's degree in English; she works at the University of Phoenix."

"She sounds smart."

"Yeah, she's smart, cool and Korean."

"What happened to the Philippine chick?"

"She was too wild and well we had a big argument and we broke up."

"Maybe you need to lay low a little bit."

"I think so. I'm worn out."

"All that fucking!" Angela said laughing.

We drove away to her apartment, parked and entered her apartment. We went to her living room.

Angela smiled and laughed and sat down on a sofa.

"I didn't know you played the bass," I said, looking at bass guitar across the room.

"I mess around a little bit."

"And you paint too?"

"Hey, I'm not just some ho in the back of the Weekly, okay."

"I can see that." I picked up the bass guitar and turned

on the small amp next to it and strummed a few strings.

"You got a nice place here. Too bad you have to leave."

"Yeah I know. I really like it, but my neighbors are so damn nosy. I mean they see all these different guys coming here and they're not stupid."

"One cool thing is that you don't have a lot of shit to move."

"Yeah but still moving is a bitch."

"I have to find an apartment too. There are a lot things that have to be done in order for this whole thing to work. I also need your help."

"Honestly I like living alone."

"I'm sure you do."

"But my neighborhood is fucked up."

"You want to smoke some weed?"

"Yeah."

"Here's your forty!" Angela handed me the forty-ounce bottle of beer and I sat back down on the floor.

Angela took out a small sack of marijuana and started to roll a joint.

"This is good shit. I shouldn't really be smoking but I like it too much."

"What's up with your acting career?"

"It's moving slow. I mean I've been staying in shape and I got an audition next week. It's actually for a Nike commercial."

"Damn sounds good!"

"I don't know. All I can do is try." Angela finished rolling the joint and lit it. She inhaled a little bit and held the smoke in her lungs and then exhaled the smoke through her nose.

I watched her.

"You like that."

"It looked really cool."

"I have a client coming over in an hour. Do you want to stick around or do you want to chill outside for a while?"

"I'll chill outside for a while," I said.

I waved goodbye to Angela and went out the front door. I had to clear my head. Again, another move had to be made. I wondered if it would be such a good idea to move in with her. Still a little high, I walked down to the campus of LACC and looked through some iron bars that surrounded the school. There in the distance was the track but farther back was the campus where I spent one summer taking a college algebra class so that I could get my diploma from college. I decided to go and walk on campus. What else could I do? Angela was on my mind. I knew her, but living with her would be a lot more complicated. At this point what did I have to lose? Then my thoughts drifted to Pauline and the sex we had and how whimsical she was and carefree but all at the same time she was cunning. How strange it was that for so long my whole impression of women had been nothing more than a fabrication. Everything I thought I knew about women was false because all the women I had been encountering were nothing like how I thought they would be, but also maybe the women I knew also felt that I was nothing like how a black man should be. Now I wanted to go back to my apartment but not before talking with Angela again. I actually liked Pauline, but I knew we could never really be in a serious relationship because she was too shallow, though at times she had little sprinkles of reality, kind of like adding some salt to your food to give it a little more taste. Seeing her again would never be the same but then again nothing has been normal for the past few days and now Angela was asking me for something I wasn't sure I was ready for. What if she wanted the same thing that Pauline wanted?

V

"I'm glad you decided to move in with me," said Angela, lighting a cigarette. She looked into my eyes. We were sitting on a park bench. She kissed me on the lips and moved her hand up my leg.

"This is so crazy," I said sighing.

"Don't worry about it," Angela said, trying to be a little bit more reassuring, but she could tell I had doubts.

"Look I'm helping you out too because you can't work until you start teaching, besides you were paying too much money over there anyway, besides screwing that crazy girl."

"I liked my old place but maybe you're right. It was time to go."

"I knew it was time for you to go and stop worrying about that Japanese chick you were dating, I'm sure she's with someone else. You're just too far apart from each other."

She pulled away from me and lit a joint and inhaled the smoke for a few seconds and then puffed on her cigarette a little bit more and then put it out. She then handed the joint to me. I took a long drag from the joint. My hair was long. Angela had braided it into cornrows.

"I like your hair. You remind me of my brother."

Angela took the joint from me and took a few more puffs before handing it back to me. She moved her hand down my leg and then pulled it back.

"Let's go look at the apartment. I have the key!" said Angela. She put on her silver-rimmed sunglasses and motioned for me to follow her to her car. We had just gotten high at Pan Pacific park.

Angela and I drove across Los Angeles. It seems like we were always driving across Los Angeles and high too. The city looked better from the inside of a car. Once you were on foot things gradually changed. There was a silence as we drove. I thought about Pauline. She had given me a photo of herself. It wasn't a really nice photo but it had her email address on it. The photographer had moved into this building a few weeks before she left. He took a few photos of me too. He didn't live there too long because he got robbed while coming home one night and that was enough to force him to look for another apartment in a better part of the city.

I thought about the postcard. It was on my desk in my apartment. It wasn't a good photo of her.

"Take this," she said. She looked into my eyes for a moment. We were on the roof. Her lipstick was bright red and seductive and she wore a white T-shirt with Arabic writing on it, tight black jeans and green Nike shoes. Gold hoop earring hung in her ears. Her lipstick just seemed so bright that it beckoned me. There was a slight pause. She then leaned toward me and we kissed. Her lipstick smeared again. It felt like we were kissing for a long time. I could feel her hands moving. She pulled away and then she just turned around and walked away through the doorway that led to the roof and disappeared down below.

Iko...

Her letters became fewer and fewer.

Iko regretted that I had decided to move into an apartment with Angela but it wasn't her life. Iko was halfway across the world so it didn't matter anymore. For now, she was a distant memory. I thought. I was wrong.

The last time I saw her was at the Los Angeles airport. It was another silent drive home from LAX. After we parked, I grabbed her bags and we caught a shuttle to her terminal. Her hair was short and black. I remembered the pictures she had sent me showing her new hairstyle. It seemed so innocent. She wrote "I love you" at the bottom of the Polaroid. She looked exactly like her mother.

Now she was leaving again. This time it would be for a long time. She took a photo of the two of us sitting on my bed. It was from a miniature Polaroid camera they didn't sell in America. I remembered how she looked at it for a while and then she crumpled it up. It made me a little sad. She tossed it on the ground, but I picked it up and uncrumpled it. I kissed her then, but she seemed sadder. There was never enough time. We had spent time on the Santa Monica Pier and in Silver Lake and stayed up all night making love until we were exhausted. Now we were at the airport. It wasn't the first time that I had seen her off. The sun was shining brightly. It was hard seeing her go. We sat and had some coffee.

"What will you do today?" she asked.

"I don't know. I have the whole day off. I think I'll just go to the beach and relax. I don't even want to think about it."

"I wish I could go with you. Don't come to Japan," she said, sipping her coffee and clasping my hand.

Soon the time came for her to leave and I walked her to her departure gate. We looked at each other for one last time. I kissed her for as long as I could. Then she tore away. She was crying but it felt like she was happy at the same time. At least it felt that way. We kept waiving to each other until she disappeared into a maze of buildings that made up the international departure terminal.

VI

I decided to move in with Angela even though I would regret it. She did like me and she was attractive, but I didn't feel the same way about her. I wouldn't have sex with her, though I thought about it and for some reason she turned on me. Maybe because I didn't want sex with her but I loved her as a friend. She had met some new girl. I didn't really like her. At one low point in the living room, I remember them both standing over me nude, while I lay on the ground with my blanket pulled over my head. Her girlfriend kicked me, but Angela pushed her back. They were egging me on to get up but I wouldn't move. Pissed off because I walked in on them fucking on the couch, after being out all night wandering the streets on mushrooms. I just wanted to run away. That was the breaking point.

Pauline moved back to Canada. That's what I had heard. I ran into her ex-girlfriend at our old building. For some reason I needed a ride home and she and her new girlfriend, who was Asian, gave me a ride to La Cienega Boulevard. It was so strange. I couldn't imagine her with a girl like that, and even though Pauline was a shallow bitch, she was cooler than this girl, but I was grateful for the ride.

"Look I know you fucked her," she said cooly.

"I knew from that moment you came to our apartment she wanted you. I couldn't trust her; that's why we broke up. It doesn't matter anymore though."

"Thanks for the ride," I said as I exited the car on La Cienega and Wilshire. I watched as the Toyota Camry drove away.

VII

The apartment was on the second floor of a ten-unit complex. It was big enough for the two of them and quiet enough not to cause anyone to be suspicious. All the units had security doors. It was strange. She opened the door slowly.

"Nice!" said Angela. She seemed relieved to finally have found a new place. West Los Angeles seemed to suit her more. I could tell. The walls were white. It was a one-bedroom apartment with a living room, kitchen and a bathroom. I would sleep in the living room on the floor. It wouldn't be hard to move everything in.

When moving time finally came. Angela had gone to a local U-Haul and had hired day laborers who were standing outside the place to help her move. I couldn't believe it. It was all done in cash and very quickly. I didn't have a lot of stuff and one guy piled it up in the living room which seemed to make Angela mad but he arranged it in a way to keep her happy temporarily. I hooked up the internet so I could answer my emails.

It would take me a few weeks to completely separate from the newspaper. I wrote and worked for a while in the accounting department long enough to get one last paycheck and then quit. I remembered I put a photocopy of my middle finger under all of the doors of all the editors who had given me trouble.

Angela...

I did do what she wanted. I waited in the kitchen a few times while she turned tricks. I sat there motionless like a spider on a web. Sometimes I just went outside but really I was supposed to be there and it got to be a bit much and it was scary as hell. I mean what was I supposed to do if something happened to her? Maybe it was just the idea of me being there that would make her feel secure, but it scared the hell out of me. I stayed high on weed and magic mushrooms and on pins and needles. Later I was homeless until my mother loaned me the money to find an apartment. I wandered the streets of West Los Angeles and especially Santa Monica, taking in foreign films late at night and smoking weed on the beach. I had finally hit rock bottom. This is not how I imagined my life after college, not after winning an award and graduating with all the fanfare. Now I was just another bum on the street.

The Palms was a crazy neighborhood. We lived in a neighborhood filled with all of these apartment buildings that were bordered by some nice suburban homes. Most of them were owned by Jews but I know there were some black people that lived sprinkled in there too. West Los Angeles was way different from living near downtown. I liked it a lot better, but I was still lonely. Iko couldn't believe what was I was doing, but well, I was on my own now. She said not to promise anything for the future and so there was nothing to believe in except myself.

It was all lies. It had taken me so long to see it but when I finally did, the nightmares stopped and my real life began while wandering the streets of Los Angeles. After Iko left, leaving the newspaper was one of the biggest moves I had made since I graduated from college, but it was something I had to do, especially since I had realized that she was never coming back and maybe everything that I thought was important to me was bullshit.

PART I

CHAPTER 1

My last dreams were about Iko and all the love we shared... nightmares that haunted my sleep. I thought I could see people, but I really couldn't see anyone and they couldn't really see me...a friend once told me not to become the Steppenwolf but because Iko was gone ... I didn't give a fuck anymore and I ate another magic mushroom.

I got this cake for my fourth birthday and it had little red and black plastic cowboys and Indians on it. Somehow the image had just stuck in my mind for a long time. I had a dream about the birthday and the cake recently. I kept seeing the little plastic men on the cake who were suspended in battle. At that time I was happy because I wasn't alone. My parents were divorced but they were together that day. I had a lot of friends around. The party was at Farrell's but that place doesn't even exist anymore. That fourth-year-birthday party was cool because I was happy and I didn't think life could be any other way. A lot of people were around and I felt secure. Now if my birthday comes and there is no party, I don't really care, though if I have a celebration that would be okay.

My father always wore these dark shades, but he had a whole lot of sunglasses. I guess because he was always breaking them or losing them. I just remember him having a lot of sunglasses and I guess that's why my sister and I like wearing them so much. I think it was to hide his eyes because he was on cocaine or weed, or just trying to be cool. He was tranquil, really chill and would be all cool and relaxed just taking it all in looking at the hips and asses of the women. Dad always made me feel cool and relaxed. I just thought of that now I had to see my father sometime soon. I should plan a trip to see him. I don't care if I had to ride a Greyhound bus or not. I missed him more than ever now.

Before, in another life, I was so lame. If only I could have been as together then as I am now. Not that I'm totally level but I'm not the nervous wreck I was in high school. Now I feel like I'm getting to know my father and myself in a new way. A way that was impossible before but maybe the same is true for him. I didn't want to fall into the cliché that things happen for a reason. There are so many things that have been ruined by my emotions. I had to kick myself sometimes. I let things just fly by me or into me. The relationship with my father is one of those things. He was someone that was more valuable to me now more than ever. There are a lot of stories written about women's relationships with their children but the relationship between fathers and sons is just as important and always will be. Now once again here was another one of those special times when I had to see him.

I become this way sometimes.

Stuck in the past.

Just thinking on an impulse.

I hallucinated on mushrooms or weed and I walked. All these thoughts were inside of my head. Sometimes I just can't stand still. Call it impulsive if you want but much of my life hardly seems like an impulse. These emotions that I have, that are so strong that they drive me insane. They're uncomfortable sometimes. I've become my own worst enemy and most of that has been due to my emotional state. I've scoured the city on just a thought, losing myself for hours and days. Sometimes it seems like years. Now I look in the mirror and realize that thought and time are one and the same. I think my father had seen something new in our relationship too.

I've imploded.

Now I was trying desperately to inflate myself back up again and it's taking some time, so that I could explode again.

Bang!

Cowboys and Indians are personas that could be any of us. At times I was an Indian attacking the covered wagons, other times it was my father. We all reverse roles sometimes. More than any of us would like to admit wrestling with our expectations. I couldn't be naiver to my own imagination. I couldn't be more Machiavellian. It's funny how a dream could change your whole day. I was left with a lot of time to contemplate my emotions, sometimes too much. I had to step out of my head, but it was hard to do.

Every day you're shooting it out with people in an illusionary way. Some days I feel like a cowboy and some days I feel like an Indian and sometimes I feel like both. My guns were totally cocked at all times. Maybe I might go someplace and have a drink and blow somebody's head off. The high-speed chases on television were runaway stagecoaches. It still looked cheesy though. I was eyeing everything from a distance in a small western town on the frontier drifting out on the landscape like a coyote. I waited high atop a bluff like Clint Eastwood looking down on unsuspecting passengers from the roof of my apartment building.

I rolled a blunt and stuck it in my mouth. Now I was feeling like Mario Van Peebles. I was feeling like Sweet Sweet Back. Night turned to day. There were fiends that existed in the day and the night. In the laundromat across the street that would pose as a saloon, a crackhead broke into coin-operated washing machines that were already broken; he was a fishing for quarters and then he would later buy a crack rock. Central American Indios, mestizos and children ran around the laundromat. An old mestizo drank vodka until he needed to cut it with water to keep from having to buy another bottle. He said people called him Cucamonga. He had been around. He told me a story about a famous prostitute in Arizona that he knew that had become a millionaire and she had bailed him out of a bad situation when he needed some money and when he was trying to get to Los Angeles. Now he's an alcoholic wasting away in front of a laundromat. I can see him on the curb in suspended animation, an inebriated mannequin. He always looked thirsty. I could see him in the laundromat drinking a fifth of vodka. The gangsters were always around, and it had all of the potential for some really fucked up situation but there was this intergalactic peace. I ate a doughnut and drank large cups of coffee filled with sugar that drifted to the bottom of the Styrofoam cup. I played soccer video games, sometimes against other opponents, who were doing their laundry. Everyone seemed to hate where I lived but it was something else to me. It was home. It suited me. It was fucked up.

Prostitutes wandered in and out of a bar across the street looking shaky and desperate and arguing with a homeless man who cleaned up the parking lot for handouts. He had dreads that were graying and he could talk fast and break you down into a molecule of street intelligence and my neighbor called him Spirit. I always gave him change when I saw him. Shopkeepers were friendly but weary. It felt like a dozen vultures would descend upon me as soon as I entered the laundromat or left my apartment. I had my six-shooter ready. I drank Cuban espressos and smoked weed. My clothes were never dried and sometimes the machines ate my quarters, but the crack fiend showed me a trick of how to get my quarters back. I looked at his hand. It had a huge gash in it. Once he put his hands around my neck because he was high on crack one day while I was writing in my journal and he was so wacked out of his head. He could have killed me right then, but he drew back like a wraith or a broken piece of glass from a bottle, stuck in flesh.

My glasses tinted automatically and I took to the streets. There were women all around with children and more on the way, young girls in jeans so tight I wondered if they could really breathe and the youths on skateboards and older Central American fathers with their families. The sun seemed intent on wielding its power. There was a lot of crazy shit happening around me all the time, little people in a big city.

Some Central American gangsters were selling crack

and trying to look like they were hanging out. Gossip ran through the saloon laundromat about someone getting busted in the motel next to my apartment building. I stayed as far away from that place as I could. The Honduran restaurant next to the bad hotel had good food but the people seemed like they only wanted to serve their own kind and they always served me the wrong dish. I felt like a stranger in my own country.

I talked to people on the street. Mathew, who was from some part of New York, talked to me about the crack scene and how if you went toward the McArthur Park at a certain time of the night you could see people with money coming into the park trying to get drugs. He said that they had a lot of money and if you had a crack pipe you could sell it for a hundred dollars. It was hard for him to walk but I would see him out there all the time and sometimes we would smoke weed right there as traffic would role by. I used to smoke weed on the stoop and people would look up and I would be smoking a joint, but Mathew stayed in the streets; he was homeless.

He knew all about the streets.

I bought collectable comic books from some old Sammy Hagar–looking rocker who was crippled from some motorcycle accident. He talked about some old club in Hollywood called the Zero Club started by Eddie Van Halen and how his father created quadraphonic sound but his idea was stolen. Maybe he was just another crackhead with stories. My heart called out for compassion but if I showed too much, I would be shot down soon in a hail of bullets. Gangster men with shaved heads and women with too much eye makeup and dyed blonde hair roamed the boulevards and everyone seemed like they wanted to be a street tough and everyone was in some type of way. We all assumed our positions and levels in the hierarchy of the streets. We all wanted the same thing. I had a college degree, hopes and dreams of becoming some famous writer. I didn't have a hungry family waiting for me to bring them worms. I didn't adorn myself with a lot of 14k gold or drive through the streets blasting music, nor did I look bourgeoisie. I only drew attention because of my hair, which looked matted and dreaded at the same time. The mestizo women distanced themselves from me on the sidewalk and on the bus or maybe they gave me curious looks trying to wonder where I was from. Nothing was normal. It just wasn't. There were no families in my apartment building and if there were, they moved out. Racist hipsters looking for apartments always asked if Latinos lived in the building with too many kids.

Every day it was the same circus, the same bandits waiting on unsuspecting settlers. I awoke early sometimes in anticipation of work. I would catch two buses and travel farther into the city, across town or downtown. Then I would arrive at some school and I was always a stranger until I had substituted sometimes there, and the children became familiar with me and liked me because I gave them a lot of freedom and spoke Spanish. They were curious about my hair and everything that I did and watched me like a hawk. I was being observed and studied and sometimes the class turned into a discussion about me. Sometimes it wasn't so easy. It was combative or near the brink of war with shouting and students being removed from the class. A young man standing inches from my face and saying, "Fuck you!" When I would go to cover another room during the day I would receive a mysterious phone call from the classroom phone and I would pick it up and "Fuck you" would be screamed at me again.

The young girls dressed too provocatively for their age and the young men were trying to be too hard. Their environment didn't allow them to be any other type of way or maybe they weren't letting themselves. Some students already had kids and what could I say about this? What could I tell a fifteen-year-old girl about life that already had size-D lactating breasts and children?

I didn't have a girlfriend, a car or a cell phone. I went out with my friends and we drank beer and liquor and talked. Women became something of a luxury, like having a nice car or a nice apartment. It seemed like everyone had gone away. The women I met were always demanding and had an indifference to my lifestyle, which put me at odds with their material instincts. I stood on top of the roof at night and looked at the Los Angeles skyline that looked like a fake movie backdrop, the type of place that I could piss on and melt into a little ball of plastic.

My grandmother saved a cowboy and an Indian from my four-year-old birthday cake. When I visited her and put my dishes in the sink, I would look at a little glass jar that held a sponge and I could see the cowboy and the Indians facing off with one another for eternity. Later it would be little green army men, but something was more appealing about the Indians and cowboys than anything else. When you played Westerns you always got to come back to life, or when you played guns. In reality you died and an ambulance came and hopefully you could cling to life long enough for them to take you to the county hospital and you might live.

There was a morning when I woke up and it was my

first day on a long-term school assignment. When I got downstairs to the lobby I found blood all over the walls and floors and there was blood in the elevator.

Day and night were one.

At that hour anything was possible. Dreams were real. There was no doubt about it. The building had become a prop downtown and my life was an even bigger facade. Blood on the concrete and life was cheap. All that could possibly happen was happening. Nothing now seemed out of the ordinary. Life rolled along like fire and water and oil. There was a war that we were all fighting each day that drew down on upon us. I kept a rap song inside of my head so long that I forgot about time. I didn't wear a watch anymore. Life became a theater and a magnifying glass by which I looked at everything in life. I couldn't escape the past even if I tried. I cried every day inside. I retraced steps occasionally, sometimes literally. Thinking back to my old elementary school field days trying to think about how I would do things differently. Here I was waiting for life to move on to the next phase. I had somehow propelled myself forward. There wasn't any other way for me to turn. I burned slowly and the fires I had kept shoveling coal into, inside of my head. What kind of cruel game was I playing with myself?

The girl in the magazine was real; she looked like Iko, only I would have missed it on Alvarado Street. I thought back again to the blood I found one morning all over the lobby of my apartment building and how the building seemed like some giant human Aztec sacrifice. There was a trail of blood that led to the basement below where I had found some books that belonged to a former tenant, who was black and had obviously worked at some old movie theater where they showed porno films before beta and VHS and who appeared to be some intellectual, renaissance invisible man. It was there that I found a cache of old black exploitation film posters. Classic editions of black literature, books by Franz Fanon in French and English and rare compilations of black poetry and poets I had never heard of. It seemed like it was meant for me to find. It sat in the basement for who knows how long. It was dusty and moldy and decaying and I salvaged what I could and returned with the lost treasure to my apartment and got lost. It seemed meant for me to find, an African-American El Dorado of classical history and culture.

I ran back upstairs in shock and called the police and then called the school to tell them I would be late. It was 6 a.m. when I found the blood and the police showed up at 7 a.m. I left the camera rolling, that I had brought down to document the horror and then they asked if I would turn it off and I said can leave it on and I did and recorded our conversation. I gave them the manager's apartment number and then I took off to work. I was late but when I got to school I was speechless. I took the train to Santa Monica Boulevard and then I boarded a bus. It was weird getting to school and seeing all these young Russian, Latino, African-American and Armenian kids looking at me and then no words would come out of my mouth and then I fell apart and told them what had happened to me that morning and they were as curious as they were horrified. I didn't know who had done it, which was a common question I was asked. I probably would never know. Strange things had happened to me like this in my neighborhood. I never stopped being shocked. I was hoping I would never become immune to what I would see because that would mean that I'm accepting it and I didn't want to accept it. It wasn't right to see prostitutes every day flashing me. To go to bed at night and hear people fucking from the bathroom window, which faced my studio apartment. To hear my neighbors fighting below who were lesbians and then they moved out and more lesbians moved in and when I woke up in the morning, I smelled Burger King chicken sandwiches coming through my window from across the street. I counted the accidents at the intersection of Third and Alvarado. I walked outside once and saw that a young Korean girl was trapped in her car and had crashed through the front doors the of Los Burritos across the street. There were just days when I didn't want to get out of bed, when I wanted to smoke a lot of weed and drink espressos and watch the sun come up and not care and turn off the phone and not have nightmares in the middle of the night thinking that I was talking to myself or screaming or talking in German, which was amusing to my college dormitory mates.

I awoke this morning with this dream about Jober's sister. I didn't really know her. That's what was so strange about the dream. It was nighttime. I was working on her mother's car or maybe I wasn't. I spoke to her while being partially covered by the hood of the car. I was trying my best to fix the car. All I could see was this massive engine and her hips. She was wearing low-cut jeans, the kind that all the girls are wearing now, and the really tight-fitting kind. Her body was peeking out on the other side the car. I saw a math book near where the battery should be underneath the hood. It looked like an old math book. There were some other objects and papers too and they didn't belong there. Everything was totally abstract. Then

I was finished. I think some papers had flown away. I spoke to her and she was really frank. We talked about things as if we had known each other for a long time. Her sunglasses were the cheesy silver reflective mirror kind. I was a little scared as well as amazed at our encounter because she's really beautiful. Then I woke up. I had an erection. I had met her only one time and she wasn't speaking English, wore tight low-midriff shiny gray pants and she moved like a salsa dancer across the room of her mother's living room.

Jober was on my mind a lot now because he had returned to Cali, Colombia. It was his sister that was in my dream this morning. It didn't seem like such a long time had passed since we had met. It now seemed like minutes but thinking about Jober's sister left a stinging sensation, like from a wasp, as well as the feeling of quick sex in my mind. But I remember Cali too and I remember getting a different sense of myself when I was there because I am African-American.

That dream was spiritual because it wasn't connected to any type of reality I know. When you have certain types of dreams somehow you just know it has a higher meaning. I realized that time had passed so suddenly now that Jober was gone and I could now easily identify our friendship. I was teaching now. I was enjoying a life that I thought wasn't possible for me years ago. My friends created the scenes and I made mental notes of all my experiences. I used to smoke joints out on the front stoop of my building and that's how we met.

"I could smell your joint all the way down the block," he said to me that day. Things would never be the same after that. I had seen him on the subway before. He looked like a traveler, rugged and nonchalant like Jack London. We met at one point that I could draw a line on so easily. He asked me the day of our meeting if I had any more pot.

"No," I said.

I told him to come back tomorrow and that I would have some more. At that time I knew Rambo. He sold all the drugs I could ever want and half of them I wouldn't need. He was a short, stocky guy from Mexico City. I had met him through another musician I use to jam with but whom Jober had cunningly asked me to leave alone so that he could have me all to himself. Rambo didn't speak much English, but he had a lot of weed and other drugs and the best prices and I thought I had found the El Dorado of weed. He didn't live too far away. He also sold heroin, ecstasy, cocaine and crack. I never took ecstasy or smoked crack;something about all that shit just didn't appeal to me. I just liked smoking pot. All we had to do was page Rambo and he would be there and have whatever we wanted. I couldn't have had it any better.

The next day Jober appeared. It was the frosting on the cake. I welcomed him in. He liked my place. "Bernal Devereaux," I said, and he introduced himself as Jober Trudeau. He gave me a few dollars and I gave him some weed. We smoked a joint. It's always nice in the beginning. I was starting to like where I was living. I took the bus to work. I was committing a Los Angeles sin but nobody noticed. I found my own sort of satisfaction.

The pot was good. I had everything I needed. It always had to be cool. When it wasn't cool it wasn't fun. I told Jober that I lived in 208 and he returned the next day. I didn't believe it. I was so open. He could have been the police. He could have been death.

"During the year 1998 I didn't smoke any weed," he said poignantly. I thought I had had a few dry spells, but for the most part I was a steady smoker. We began to talk often, always about Colombia, mostly in his apartment. Later we moved to the fourth-floor balcony and then to the roof.

I always tried to be optimistic, but my expectations of people and situations and I was too high and that made me naive. Then I found myself in Cali, Colombia. Of all the places in the world where one could find oneself and everybody was telling me not to go. My father told me that if I saw any suspicious drug lab then I should tell my friends that I had to go home. Others were more inspiring.

I didn't want to think that I was running away. My job was giving me the blues and so I knew it was time to resign. I felt for the children I was leaving behind. I was teaching special education at an inner-city school. A student in my class had assaulted a female classmate. I grabbed him and threw him out of the room. I got in trouble for it. I almost lost my ability to teach. I'm glad that I resigned because I can't stand betrayal. I felt so betrayed. So, I bought a ticket, sold my car and flew to Cali, Colombia. I ran away. Teaching was important to me, but I was living a dual life. I was a teacher by day and an artist by afternoon and night. On the weekend it was worse. I knew a lot of people but for the most part I was on the outside of life in the city looking in. It happened in spurts. I was trying really hard to make something happen. I bought a ticket and Cali was only the thought in my head. I had to escape.

I couldn't wait. My mouth was watering. I couldn't stop jacking off. I felt like I was fourteen. I masturbated four times a day. When I worked at the paper, it was worse. I was so exhausted afterward but the emotion is so great I feel like I'm going to burst. No woman was free from my imagination. If I saw a girl and I liked her, I had fantasies of fucking her. On the bus, in the metro, in the classroom, on the sidewalk—it didn't matter where. The urge was too great to resist. Then sometimes I felt nothing. I was numb. I couldn't even move my dick. Springtime and summertime were worse. Iko couldn't take it. I fucked her into unconsciousness. She didn't want to be fucked that hard. She would start getting loud and then I would cum. Now I just had to jack off. I wondered if there was a limit or if there was such a thing as jacking off too much.

Jober liked porn. He pondered the thought of his ex-roommate girlfriend watching him jack off. He thinks she saw him do it. That's one of my fears of masturbating—getting spied on. But those types of thoughts make you feel even more depraved.

The window to Jober's room had been at an angle and he heard a tap at a window, meaning that his roommate's girl didn't have her key. Then he went outside when she was gone to check the logistics from where she was when she hit the window. Bull's-eye—she could see everything, he thought, so he had to assume she had seen him. I asked him if he knew how long she might have been standing there and he didn't know. Fuck-it but then you have that feeling of being violated.

Time became irrelevant.

I always thought it would be different. It was funny how thoughts became reality and I was living my imagination. When Jober and I would meet daily after we finished working, all he talked about was Cali and his life as a punk rock musician. About heroin at fourteen, sleeping with prostitutes, good weed and more punk rock music, passing out on Rizatriptan. It sounded cool and I lost brain cells listening to him and but I couldn't get enough.

"You've got to go to Cali," said Jober. Somehow things always came down to that statement. I was a good listener. I gleaned every word he spoke. We smoked weed and swapped stories and the city was the stage for our misadventures. It wasn't real. It could have been a dream. When you're permitted to step outside of your life it all looks different but it all looks the same too. I was pissed every day. I couldn't keep my marbles anymore. I was emotionally deteriorating from teaching. It was my first full-time teaching job at a middle school. I had experienced everything emotionally that a teacher could experience except sex. Teaching was tough. I loved it. I tried to make the most of it. In the end I asked Jober where to buy a ticket to Cali.

"Pan-American at Sunset and Alvarado," he quipped. I was always somehow connected with Latin America. It's in me too. We had talked about Cali so often. The only thing we were missing was plane tickets. I loved good stories and I loved adventure. It's cool when you could have both and some people experience it all at an earlier age than others but that doesn't make them better people, it just makes them more experienced. I considered his friends to be more expats than foreigners. They would return home sometimes, others wouldn't. That's something that Jober knew a little more about than me.

It seemed that as crazy as I was, I was doing the right thing. Jober asked me one day how I could have stayed in school for so long and for me it was simple. What else was there for me? I wanted to be a famous writer. Jober had seen the other side but he had landed in Spain and had found that his friends had found other forms of escape, strung out on ecstasy, and that there was no turning back for them. Colombia was truly far and fewer in between. Jober could return but for the others life awaited them outside. The decades of civil war at home would take years to conclude and then would life ever be the same? If there was some insane solution to the problems facing Colombia it looked like life was going on as usual in Cali but in reality it wasn't. But what were people supposed to do? The expressions on the soldiers and the graffiti on the walls that stretched en masse along the landscape showed a completely different picture than what we all wanted to believe. In a state of war, life moves forward regardless of terror that surrounds the people. It's funny how even death and destruction, turmoil and frustration can make one insensitive. That's when we find that as humans, we were like any other creatures that exist. We were cold blooded and cruel and made life seem as cheap as crushing an ant under one's New Balance running shoes. The stories were endless, the little forms of resistance, but the escalation of chaos and the almost humorous ways in which such brutality has been acted out by its participants made it seem like a dream.

South America seemed like Tom Sawyer's island on cocaine, after hearing Jober speak. I wanted to go but it just wasn't the right time yet. If I only knew how soon I would be there in the tropical sun looking at low-midriffs-jeans-wearing novella models. I was constantly in unknown territory. I somehow winged my trip later but not without scars. Nothing in life comes easy. I should have been aware of that by now. I knew that for every frosted cake there could be something distasteful underneath. I was looking for that. I had short perception. I really did. But I just lived life sometimes thinking that I didn't have to think about certain things. Who wanted to think about racism or class or failure?

Pornography

Jober loved porn and he loved to talk about it. Somehow pornography was as natural as watching *Friends* on television. When we communicated, we had certain openness. Everything was fair game. It wasn't always fair. Sometimes it was ego. Sometimes it was racist.

"I taught this ESL class today and this girl showed me this picture she printed from the internet of some woman sucking a man's dick! I couldn't believe it. Diablitas!" I said.

"I saw them later on my way home from the school. I didn't expect to see them. I boarded the bus with my head down. I was tired. Then I heard someone call 'Teacher!' I looked up and it was the girl who had the picture in class. She told me to sit next to her. I was a little reluctant to but then I sat on a seat in front of hers. She was with her friend. They both had the dirty pictures in class of the women performing fellatio on men. I didn't know what to say to them. They were both Latinas. One of them had a lot of acne on her face, especially the one who liked me. If

I had to choose one of them, it would have been her friend. Suddenly their stop came up and then they said bye and exited the bus but not before one of their friends pushed her into me. Her breasts rubbed against me. She seemed a little embarrassed but politely said sorry and exited the bus. I can't fuck a high school girl!" Jober laughed.

"I felt a little awkward. I mean, I looked in the trash later after they had left class and I examined a piece of the picture printout that one of them had thrown away. It was picture of a woman sucking a man's dick. I was shocked that those girls could be so daring, so young. It seemed almost normal for them. Maybe I was just very conservative. Maybe I was fucking stupid!"

It was just the type of thing Jober liked to talk about.

"Don't women know what they're doing to you when they wear tight clothes? It's funny how women behave as if you're not going to look at them. If you see an attractive woman you're going to look her body," said Jober smiling.

"Lips, tits and hips," said Jober.

He was always drinking water and he was now filling himself a glass of distilled Sparklet's Water. Something about the tropics had made him that way. Los Angeles was dry. You felt it and Jober's necessity for water confirmed it. I could tell that he loved women. He was intrigued by their design and he put them on a pedestal. Porn was the ideal, like owning a pet. In porn one found the perfect woman. The woman never complained and never looked ugly but real life was harsh and the worst thing being you could be rejected. With porn one could be a conquistador.

Jober spared nothing. Not long after I had known him I had visited his apartment. We probably spent about equal time in both our places. But his place always brought the fire out of us. He was quite a photographer and he had a huge portrait of his sister in his living room. Somehow I couldn't stop looking at that picture no matter how hard I tried to steer clear of it.

"I remember when my sister had a boob job!" he said rather candidly one day. I didn't know what to say. I hadn't even met her.

"After her operation I saw her lying there in the bed and I went and took my finger and poked one of her boobs. She was sort of bandaged up," he said solemnly. Jober's sister was beautiful and he knew it; so did she.

I could see the disbelief on his face and in his words. I wondered what he thought about me. In my dream I spoke to Jober's sister the way I spoke to him in reality. Alvarado was my Nesky Avenue that Gogol and Dostoevsky described in such detail in their novels. This reality seemed impossible but so was going to Cali, Colombia. At least Brazil would come first, I thought.

Smoking weed out on the fourth-floor balcony was cool. After Jober's living room, that was our favorite place to talk. He was loud and spoke without discretion. He was a one hundred percent Colombian. I was more discrete, and that's what he perceived as my strange style of conservatism, but we could talk about anything. I had started smoking pot at eight years of age and he was doing heroin at fourteen and playing in a punk rock band called Los Rudas, around Cali. His father was a businessman but he was also a narco-trafficker, a gentlemen trafficker. I didn't find out about the drug part till later but it still wouldn't have made me feel different about who Jober was. And I'm sure after I resigned from my teaching job because a student had attacked me with a chair, which I had kicked back at him after he assaulted a girl in the classroom and that he might see me as a little crazy. But he wasn't in the classroom and I could sense those scenes bouncing around in his head. We had a delicate friendship. It was on thin ice. I didn't trust a lot of people and I know that he felt the same way too. I think I was a little too trusting. But what is friendship? I didn't really know. It's a gut feeling you go with. Friends fight and that's something that people don't really talk about. His dad was in Vietnam. His parents met at UC Berkeley and then drove in an old Dodge Palomar police car to Cali, Colombia. You can't get any more daring than that. Our families had crossed paths, we felt, somewhere in the past Bay Area Tower-of-Power scene. We were sure of it and well maybe we hit the mark more than our relatives had. There was some sort of providence in it all and we rode on it. The other aspects of our lives weren't so synergetic. We were worlds apart in class and race. We loved James Brown, beautiful women, Bad Religion and De La Soul. Between us we were of different ethnicities and races, though he was part white and I was part black, but my mother was Creole by way of New Orleans and his father was a mestizo from Colombia, but we were both of French extract. His mother was from a wealthy wasp California family from Tennessee, former slave owners. I was from a working-class bourgeois African-American and Creole-French background but I was college educated and working toward joining the intelligencia, however I definitely wasn't rich.

Jober was a rock and roller. He lived it and now life had once again brought him to America but when he left he had become something grotesque. He liked Sublime, the Ramones and Screeching Weasel. I liked everything but country music. I was no stranger to punk, but he was punk unlimited. He loved what I listened to and our parents had similar tastes in music. We even played music together before egos turned our emotions into pit bulls. It's always fun in the beginning. It wasn't easy being Bernal Devereaux around him. We were both at odds with society, social outcasts, stoners but proud of it.

CHAPTER 2

Mercedes Bello Veracruz was an elderly Cuban woman living in exile in Los Angeles, California. She was my only true confidant. She was also a Sephardic Jew, sixty-six years old, though she looked half her age and was an Afro-Cuban artist. I met her during my undergraduate years of college. Somehow, again, fate had brought me to this woman.

My mother thought Mrs. Veracruz was attracted to me. I thought Mrs. Veracruz was one of the most interesting people I knew. It seemed like she had done it all. She met Hemingway in Havana, Cuba. He propositioned her for sex but she declined. "I'm not a prostitute," she said to him.

"Then what are you?" he asked.

"I'm an artist," she replied.

He bought her a drink and left. Stories like that captivated me and she had a lot of them. When I wasn't with Jober I was with Mrs. Veracruz. She had a lot of troubles. The first being her husband, Roberto Veracruz, an ex-pachuco from the zoot suit era. Only Edward James Olmos could have done a better job at portraying him. Mr. Veracruz was dying of cancer. He now had a colostomy bag attached to his body but he could still get around and he was still as frank and cunning as he was when we he was gangbanging way back in the early 1940s. Now he has a bachelor's degree in art, talks to children about the importance of education and art and how to stay out of gangs.

"Los Angeles was so racist then," he told me once, "and it still is!" Mr. Veracruz had seen the worst and the best of Los Angeles but now he was dying. Mrs. Veracruz loved him and she did her best to make him feel comfortable even though she complained about his machismo ways. I was always there to listen, always.

They were my friends and I had traveled with them across the Los Angeles landscape, meeting artists and intellectuals, African-American and Latino, rich and poor. When I was with them I felt more like a Latino. My Spanish was not that good but I had learned to comprehend as well as speak better Spanish being around them. With Jober it was different, though I think he saw me as being something other than African-American, maybe because my mother was Creole-French.

Mrs. Veracruz was Creole too, but not like Creole-French. The ethnic makeup of Cuba I would later learn was so similar to New Orleans that the two places might as well have been the same place. Mrs. Veracruz's parents were descendants of Sephardic Jews who had immigrated to Cuba. Her father raised Arabian horses on the island. Her mother's parents were merchants. In the colonies people tend to stick with their own kind sometimes.

At sixteen Mrs. Veracruz left her home in Santiago and went to Havana. She told me all she had was fifty cents in her pocket. Enough to take a bus to the city but she couldn't find work. A pimp approached her immediately. She was young and beautiful, thin and white skinned. That makes a big difference to Creoles, French or other. She thought he was just trying to pick her up but what he really wanted was to use her to make a lot of money. The pimp had a car. They went out and went for a drive, he tried to make a move and she slashed his face with a razor and fled back to town.

Havana was exciting but it was also very dangerous, especially for a sixteen-year-old girl with nice curves. It wasn't a nice place for Jewish girl from the provinces. That night she slept in a Catholic church. The next day she found a job at a restaurant, but it was filled with prostitutes. The owner of the restaurant gave her a room upstairs. She learned fast.

"I sniffed coke . . . wow . . . it made me so paranoid," Mrs. Veracruz told me one day. I couldn't believe it but then I had done it myself and the day she told me about using cocaine I had a severe sinus problem. She asked me in Spanish if I was using cocaine. I said no but she knew that I had used it before.

"I tried heroin too . . . I know you know about that stuff too," she said with a grin.

I had tried heroin a few times and I would try it again with Jober too but I never used a needle.

Havana was Las Vegas before Fidel Castro took over. It was filled with casinos, gangsters, playboys and playgirls. Mrs. Veracruz was there and she saw it all. The restaurant job was tough and the conditions weren't the best but she made the most of the situation. Mr. Parti, the owner, was kind but shrewd. Then one day it happened. Another man came along except this time he wasn't a pimp but a general in Batista's army. He had a nice car, a convertible. He talked sweet. He knew that Mrs. Veracruz was a Sephardic Jew like himself. They didn't go to synagogues and most of the Sephardic were Catholic converts. After giving him a hard time, she decided to go out with him. It couldn't get any worse and if he tried anything, well she had a straight razor in her purse. Hopefully she wouldn't be needing it and they had dinner at a nice restaurant near the ocean. It was an expensive place and she knew that he had money and he knew that she was in a desperate situation. At this time Mrs. Veracruz could get what she wanted because she was young and beautiful but she had the intellect to go along with it.

Samuel Aguirre came from a wealthy Havana family. His father was a judge and so was his father before him. Mrs. Veracruz had found her man and Mr. Aguirre had found his woman. Soon they were married. Mrs. Aguirre, as she was now known, was living in a palatial mansion. Cinderella would have been jealous of the crystal chandeliers, marble floors. She had a chauffeur and maids. Her parents didn't approve of her marriage but she had left home a long time ago. Now she was a grown woman, not a naive girl fresh from the Cuban countryside. She was going to school and studying art. There were frequent trips to Puerto Rico and Venezuelan art schools and a short vacation to Miami or New York. It was a fairytale life. The only thing missing was a carriage with white horses and a prince.

I saw the pictures and I couldn't believe that it was true until I saw the photos of the crystal chandeliers. I saw the pictures of her with the sub-machine gun in her hands as she stood in the back of a jeep one day on a trip to one of the outlying provinces. Again, I had found someone with stories that rivaled the comic book tales that overshadowed my youth. In each of those tales about her life was a lesson. Lessons that were painful and lessons that I knew all too well because I was in a lot of emotional pain every day like a junkie.

I never knew when Mrs. Veracruz would bring up the past. But every day she seemed to be reliving it. She would look at old black and white photos of herself of when she was young and beautiful and not so wrinkled and more desirable. When men wanted her and she knew why they wanted her and she could get what she wanted from them as well and how it all made her feel and that she had to come to terms with the fact that now she was an older woman living a more modest lifestyle, light years away from the austere life she led on the island of Cuba, long ago, when she was the envy of most women and most of the Cubans, who were now presently living in poverty, a reality that has now become so much a part of her life.

In the past she said that Mr. Aguirre would say, "Teach him how to pray!" Which only meant that some poor Cuban who had fallen into the arms of the law was to be tortured or executed. Who knows what horrors those were but one could only imagine that it could have been any horror that is as real today as it was then. Sometimes an old picture could bring up a long-buried memory. I listened to it all. There was no way that I couldn't. She lived the life that many of us only dream about, as cliché as that may seem. Especially here in Los Angeles, which is saturated with so much money and people parading around their materialism. But when I think of people living "rich" I thought about her life, not Beverly Hills, or someone in a Mercedes Benz. Everyone had a Mercedes now, but nobody had lived like Mrs. Veracruz had once lived. Her husband also worked for Meyer Lansky.

There was another reason why I was close to Mrs. Veracruz and that was because she also believed in Santeria. She was devoted to it. She had been initiated at an early age in her small provincial town and those people she protected her. Her parents were racist and adhered to the strict segregation of the races in Cuba. Barriers, which exist even to this day, even in the United States. I mean, we all live together to a certain degree but we're not really together, at least some of us aren't. Santeria was in all of her art and it was a part of her life, more than Catholicism or Judaism. This was of interest to me too because it was both interesting and mysterious. It was also very African and I was always in search of ways to stay in touch with my own culture and understand it. Santeria was something that had survived through slavery in the Americas. That's how powerful it is and will always be. I was sort of apprehensive about it in the beginning and though I'm not initiated I could have been taken to certain places and met those who are. I've contemplated really being a part of it and I'm sure I will be someday. I wear green and black beads around my neck that represent Ogun. In my neighborhood there are so many Botanicas and though some of these places may be genuine I could also see in it the commercialized side of the religion but what religion doesn't hand people a commercialized version of it? Well, I was hooked and I was hooked on Mrs. Veracruz and her stories and her fairy tales.

I was also living my own fantasy and though I spent so

many afternoons with Mrs. Veracruz and her husband Mr. Veracruz I had to return to my own reality. That I was a substitute teacher eking out a living in an enormous sprawling city that devoured its best inhabitants. That I was alone and was in desperate need of someone that would understand me, but such a person could not be found.

My friends were my comfort and Mrs. Veracruz and I bonded over our mutual need for understanding. Our birthdays were on the same day and we celebrated them together on several occasions. It was shocking to know that one's life could be in such parallel to another's. That in some way there was this synergy that existed in the universe and revealed itself in so many creative ways that it was beyond anyone's understanding. That a woman like Mrs. Veracruz could have been born on an island on the same day as me and have the same types of feelings and regrets and joyful experiences as my own. That I sometimes wish that she wasn't so old but young like myself so that we could share so much more. But that would be too perfect and such a reality doesn't exist and I could only dream about it like I dreamt about Jober's sister who parades around in my dreams like a novella star or some other woman that I couldn't probably get as close to unless I was watching Univision.

My meeting with Mrs. Veracruz always ended with a ride home in her old yellow Toyota Tercel, the same make and model of a car that I too once owned, or I returned home alone on a bus or a train thinking about what type of day had expired. About how cunning Mr. Veracruz is and his calm reserve, which only makes him more mysterious. His tales of zoot suit riots and life and imprisonment in Leavenworth Prison for hitting an officer because he insulted his mother and his later travels to Chicago and New York where he met up with other gangster types like himself. I could only dream of such a life compared to the bizarre life I was leading, a life that could easily be boring but was really fueled by my desire to find the truth, in the midst of my chaotic life, in an unscrupulous city.

CHAPTER 3

Now I just felt like I was going nowhere. The nightmares that I had been having had become worse and worse. I had finally visited Japan and it was in Japan that the nightmares began, about three years ago. I had to sleep in a separate room from Iko because we weren't married. There were only four of us at Iko's house, her mother, brother, who wanted to get prostitutes but neither of us had any money. I was still having these bad nightmares. Each dream was different but the effect was the same. I woke up feeling that I had screamed and everyone had heard me. It was a silent scream but so terrifying that I could remember every detail for a few seconds after opening my eyes. The second nightmare was the one that had penetrated my soul. I woke up with the same screaming feeling and then I pushed away the covers and the tatami and went into the bathroom with the electronic toilet and looked in the mirror. I had a pimple growing on my forehead and I wanted to be sleeping with Iko, not alone. I put some water on my face and I went to bed. Then I had another nightmare. They didn't stop and I told Iko's mother about them at breakfast. She feigned interested about my dreams, except for the ones that were real. What was material seemed more important to her. I didn't really trust her but she had a good sense of humor. She was friendly but behind her smile was one of cunningness that she had passed on to her able daughter. I felt like I should have said something to get even with her when I had the chance but I was too insecure. When she had come to America and she had told Iko that she needed a man with money, the kind of man that could pay for her to stay at the Beverly Hills Hotel and afford her the life that she felt she had or deserved.

Class consciousness was the furthest thing from my mind but I guess that it was my naiveté to believe that she could be sincere. I guess that's why Iko and I took off across southern Japan. We couldn't stay at her house; it just seemed better to get away. I just told myself that I would make the most of the trip and that I wouldn't let any of it get me down. How to be gracious in the line of fire? Iko was just as cunning as her mother and after one night of having sex with her in my apartment, I had a dream that I was really fucking her mother and that they had made a switch only because her mother wanted to see what I was really like. I didn't think they could be so diabolical but so many things had been proven otherwise, but our love was perverted and I was lost. I loved my trip to Japan and I didn't have any money when I arrived and this made Iko furious but I had made it, after eleven hours, I had made it. Japan was intense and I saw seven cities, in two weeks, but I didn't see Iko's father, who objected to her being with me and Iko's mother told me what I already knew. We're not together anymore so it doesn't matter. She told me I was told not to have any promises about the future. That meant that we were not going to be together for long. That it was really over between us.

It was gradual.

It was in slow motion.

I didn't know how to comprehend it. Nothing had prepared me for all of this. So, I drank my coffee and I was trying hard to recover from my nightmares and Keiko, Iko's mother, hands me a cutout of an article from a Japanese newspaper. The article was about a young white guy, twenty-seven, who had just written a book. He was inspired by Yukio Mishima, an author I had idolized for so many years. I was happy and I felt I was connecting with Iko's mother but I knew I needed to have money to be with her daughter and I had none and so nothing had changed.

Keiko was happy. She had a house in Chiba, Prefecture, Japan. It was suburbia, and with that came a Jaguar car, playing golf with her friends and she didn't work except a few hours a day at a golf shop. Her children, they were her only disappointments in her life and mainly Iko's brother but both of them were good kids, I had concluded. The last time I met Iko's mother was when I was in college. She asked me how old the United States was and I almost bungled the answer. I had never been approached that way but the tricky nature of Iko only confirmed where it had all sprung from. I flashed back to Keiko's kitchen in a Chiba suburb. She listened to Billy Joel: "What's a matter with the car I'm driving ...." I think I knew the rest of the song but it sort of suited her self-centered, almost yuppie, persona. There was breakfast. An ad for a job for her son and his cigarettes she had bought for him. I wanted to forgive her at that moment for our first meeting. Decisions had already been made.

When she was visiting Iko in Los Angeles, her mother

did not attend my graduation, but Iko was there with her friends, smiling because "I have a future and talent!" She said kissing and hugging me. Unfortunately I had chosen one of the hardest professions in the world, writing. I wrote to Iko and told her about my insomnia before arriving in Japan, which I had developed because of my fear of failure. The nightmares were driving me crazy. I tried to deal with the situation positively. She didn't seem to care.

Fighting, dreams of death and Iko running away from me, losing me while running through some temple and up steps and then, not being able to catch her. Dreams of Iko sleeping with one of my friends, but I've blocked that out of my mind, I think. The nightmares persisted and I became a nervous paranoid wreck. I wrote an email to Iko and told her on the phone about what was happening to me and she listened but she wanted to know if I was moving to a better apartment in a better part of the city.

In Japan things had not been much different. I arrived a little tired and not knowing what to expect but telling myself the whole time to have a good time no matter what, only realizing now that I was being devoured. That house. I liked where they lived and people seemed happy but Dad was gone and the repeated message was for her to marry someone Japanese and rich, not black. I had come so far in my life and been through too much to let that bother me but maybe my denial of reality only made me more naive.

That last time I saw Iko I should have known it was the end. I thought she would actually come back. It was a strange day. We were in the rental car. Her friend had left a few weeks earlier and almost caused a disturbance when she took off her shirt in my living room with her back facing me, tempting me. I rushed to the bathroom as quickly as I could but Iko busted in thinking I had been aroused but they both wanted to have sex with me.

I didn't know it then but when I saw Iko that last time we were really saying goodbye to each other. Then sometimes I felt like it wasn't a goodbye but a fuck-you. She wore some sort of lingerie that she had bought when we first met. She gave me a blowjob and I should have known where everything was going. It was so strange how money had been the most pressing matter but now that I was making decent money our relationship had ended.

Leaving the newspaper was symbolic of the end of some chapter in my life. It had started so sweet. I had been so excited. I had enjoyed so many pleasures and pains from being in the paper. I won't mention its name but it's well known. Seeing young talented writers mired in the "Pit" where we fact-checked stories for other writers who somehow seemed to excel beyond belief. It was competitive. Still I felt I had been stymied. A disk of my stories had disappeared. Stories were never printed. This was devastating to me. To make matters even more bizarre one of my best friends who happened to be some sort of escort was fucking one of the editors of the paper. I was convinced when my friend had shown me a copy of the book he had written and autographed for her. I didn't believe her until one day she came to the paper to pay for one her ads.

"I'm fucking one of your editors," she said before getting into her BMW and driving away leaving me on the curb on Sunset.

Shit!

I was stuck for a moment. Thinking back to when I was

working in the accounting department, checking ads, shredding papers, and Shonna the crazy Filipino girl who couldn't seem to get enough sex despite her large collection of DVD porn, given to her by a friend who was a porn movie reviewer.

Something had happened to me.

I had developed a fetish. There were things that I didn't think about. Details that I had missed. I could see it now in another type of way. I just had to think about it in a more positive way. I thought about her a million times and I looked at her a million ways while making love to her. How diabolical Iko could be. It was unimaginable and classic at the same time. Iko made everything melt. I became a birthday cake in front of her. She took the pieces she wanted. I had changed her too. There was something about her that had captivated me. Not even going all the way to Japan and across its islands was enough to bring us together. I had become obsessed and depressed.

Then everything changed again. I was able to go to sleep again. I remember for almost three days. These dreams were different. They were about Hada, from Tehran, Iran, to be exact. She was the first girl, I think, that I could call my girlfriend or really wanted to. It was in high school. We never touched each other but once, and if I knew then what I know now, I would have taken things a step further. It happened suddenly and sweetly but all my dreams began to be about Hada and the budding relationship that we had before I had moved from Northern California to Southern California. I missed her and I know she missed me but like everything in my life, she had become only a memory, a short painful psychedelic memory.

Recently I had been fired from the largest alternative weekly newspaper in Los Angles, but that was the least of my troubles. On my last day I photocopied my middle finger and put it under the door of all of writers and editors I felt had done me wrong. My girlfriend, Iko, was thousands of miles away, so I pined away; I idolized and worshipped her and here I am left with my angry thoughts of her. I grew my hair long and smoked marijuana every day. Sometimes I was lost on magic mushrooms. I took mushrooms for weeks. How I wanted Iko and dreamed of her every night but every day feeling further and further away. I would do anything to have her back. Whatever I could think of to show her my affection and love, I would send it to her. She never wrote back. My correspondence with her became less and less, until I found myself writing to myself. Maybe I had been too selfish and too foolish.

What had I really given her?

These long-distance relationships can devour your soul. I still didn't feel reconciled from her brusqueness, how she had injured me after sex, only out of frustration, her hand hitting my cheek. She had even pulled a knife on me but I took it away from her. She was violent at times but maybe that was due to violence that had been perpetrated against her. If I recall, an ex-boyfriend had kicked her out of bed once, really hard, hurting her. People kept asking me why I was wasting my time with her but that was a question I should have been asking myself. I think later she had asked herself the same question which eventually did lead to the end of it all, an ex-hostess who lost her virginity to an American service man at sixteen.

I kept wondering what I had done wrong. I guess my problems with her began when she realized that time was running out and that she would soon have to return home to Japan. The pressure began to rip us apart. There was always a sense of urgency. Nothing was right after that. It was all about communication but I didn't buy the violent reactions because I knew she was a lot more articulate then she let on.

Our relationship started off slow and nice but then turned so wrong and I kept wondering what had gone wrong. What had happened to us? Why had we come to this?

I couldn't have been more immature and attached and she couldn't have been more shallow and if only I could have said no or let go at the right time. I had run too much with the spinning top on the playground and now that it was moving, I couldn't let go or completely get on it or get off.

I cheated on Iko after returning from Japan because I was so frustrated. I had a chance with this new girl after I let her edit a book I was trying to write. She was more concerned with sex than my book, but she did help me notice some errors in my novel. We eventually broke up. It ended like it began.

"I can't believe I gave you head!" she said to me at work one day, looking me in the eyes. She walked away from me like she wanted to cry.

Shonna was the one who approached me at work first, with Post-its that said, "Let's fuck!"

Iko had told me not to promise anything for the future. I felt unleashed afterward. If I had been smarter, I would have let her go a long time ago, but distance had done that. But I loved her, even though now I had become a Steppenwolf.

So Shonna, the nymphomaniac from my newspaper job, and I hung out together and I never touched her except once, and but then we kissed and she stroked me and then two weeks later we fuck at 3 a.m. She puts on a pink bra and performs oral sex. I put my hands on her head as it moved up and down until I came in her mouth. We took a shower and she poured some soap in her hand and made me look at it and smiled because it looked like cum. We could only sleep for a few hours because we had sex so late at night and we would have to get up and go to work the next day. We were totally exhausted. I felt like I was on a roller coaster. She was so tight I couldn't even get it inside of her. It wouldn't be too long before she would be leaving to the Philippines to visit some relatives and do photography.

She smiled at me at work. I looked forward to seeing her every afternoon. I walked my own dog to her place in the middle of the night up Vermont Boulevard. She offered me water and we would sit down together or maybe outside on her front porch when it was hot. She might put in one of her porno DVDs and giggle a little bit. Her roommate was equally voluptuous and left her bra on the couch one day. It looked like it could fit over my head. I sat down for dinner one afternoon and her roommate gave me a metal ring. I asked her what it was for and she said it's a cock ring to make my dick stronger. I asked her if we were being too loud and she said she couldn't hear us.

Sometimes we smoked pot out on her porch. Shonna had a dog named Woody who seemed to have attention-deficit disorder. The nymphomaniac with hair like Sean Young's from Blade Runner, and she actually posed for a friend of hers who was a photographer trying to recreate a scene from the movie. She had exotic pipes that she had somehow gathered from different parts of Asia and we tried to smoke out of a different one each time, every night.

For a moment I felt like I was in paradise. Hanging out at this strange house in Silver Lake with two voluptuous women smoking weed every day if not before work. I couldn't have been any higher. Those nights walking around the Silver Lake reservoir talking with her, kissing her against the fence, I pulled up her skirt and she wasn't wearing any underwear. A car came and flashed its lights. We took off running before the car could turn around. That was too close.

I let her read my book and the next thing you know we're fighting. My fling had told me that she had certain needs and one night after I refused to fuck her she took my finger and placed it between her legs. Then she wanted me to masturbate, so she could watch but I said no. She had to get off at any cost. She had told me that while I was in Japan she fucked another black guy across street, an aspiring rapper that had just recently signed to Grand Royal, the Beasty Boys' independent record label. It's now defunct. It didn't take this girl long and I had held out as long as I could. Things couldn't have been more opposite between us. She was a trendy Silver Lake vintage type who used to just smoke Marlboros and talk about life and the alternative paper where we worked. I felt she was so out of touch. She had stacks of DVD porn and she would watch them and complain about there not being enough penetration. She was really a perverted punk rock girl who grabbed my dick and said she wanted to fuck and that she would tell me when to stop. I felt like we could fuck anywhere, like animals.

Women are always on a timeline. Finish college at twenty-one, career and a baby at twenty-five and then a house at thirty. This girl had it all planned out. She had broken up with her boyfriend and had graduated from Cal State Long Beach and was originally from Azusa, not far from the landfill. She broke up with her long-time Filipino boyfriend. It seemed that she had done what Mommy and Daddy wanted but now she had become a nymphomaniac and wanted to get fucked hard from black guys. She liked fucking and her pussy was shaved and it was really tight and when I put it in she screamed out the window and I heard somebody laugh outside on the street.

I thought Shonna was Mexican when I first saw her but she was Filipina and a Filipina princess at that. She drove a 1962 or was it a '63, white Fleetwood Cadillac and lived in Silver Lake. She was definitely a Silver Lake girl and her roommate was a sister with size-F breasts. These girls were crazy and would make a lot of food and would invite all of their friends over and would drink and socialize. I couldn't complain. I had my hair braided then and posed with a trumpet for some art assignment by her Hollywood photographer friend in Silver Lake.

One night I met some of her friends and afterward we drank and after taking shots of tequila one night we ran through the hills of Silver Lake with her dog, who was really hyperactive, and we ended up at a used book and record store and I was stuck there for hours looking for old LPs. I was so drunk and as we walked to the store, I revealed little secrets about myself like going to county jail and the fact that my mother had gone to jail too. I thought that was enough. She really just wanted to fuck me and I knew now for sure that women were just like men and that everything that I thought about relationships between men and women was wrong. It only made matters worse because I was trying my best to survive. It was my dream to write and now it looked like everything was going crazy. I kept telling myself that I only wanted to concentrate on my writing.

I fucked Shonna and she screamed bloody loudly like Iko when we had first done it. Both of them sounded like ambulance sirens. I knew now my first book was lost somehow when Shonna didn't react to the racial content that I was trying to discuss. She just didn't get it. I was so frustrated with her. We just fucked. I liked Shonna but we were moving in different directions like Los Angeles freeways.

I wasn't Silver Lake. . . . I was from another planet. I didn't mind the whole hip scene but I wasn't a part of it, just an interloper. The cars were cool and well they could look at me and think that I was wack too. The whole thing ended with me walking home with my book back home in the middle of the night and she watching me from her porch as I got farther and farther away. Shonna quit the newspaper after returning from the Philippines to do some photography. I liked Shonna a lot but we were too hot. Iko was in New York. That was it.

I wouldn't have no bullshit with Iko, none of it, except that I should have told her to get the hell out of my life. I kept trying to give Iko a chance but I was lying to myself. Now it's done because she'd finally gone to New York and was not coming to see me. I remembered again after meeting Iko's mother for the first time after putting her and her mother in my 1982 Toyota Tercel and whisking us off to Beverly Hills, where we were fortunate enough to see Jackie Chan, smoking a cigar with a friend at the entrance to Rodeo Drive, then Iko's mother and I walked across the street to the Beverly Wilshire Hotel to go to the bathroom. "They filmed *Pretty Woman* here," she said. I didn't know and I didn't care; I couldn't stand Julia Roberts.

Later Iko revealed to me that her mother felt she should be with someone who had more money. She said she defended me by saying that I had paid for my college education on my own. But how much of what she was telling me was the truth? I was mad as hell when I heard this and I wanted to confront her mother but I decided against it and I told myself I shouldn't' worry about it. What else do I expect from a woman who, after I had just met her, came and stood next to me because I'm much taller than both of them, measured her foot against mine and then looked at Iko, who then grimaced.

Everything in our relationship revealed to me that we were opposites. Then she gave into me. Why? If only to get me to work harder and earn more and I had to. I was stuck trying to fill a bottomless pit. Trying to buy a Tiffany bracelet or a Louis Vuitton purse. I was starting to feel less guilty. The straw that broke the camel's back was when Iko told me that her father didn't' want her to marry a foreigner. She couldn't marry a nigger. It didn't matter how much education I had or how much money I made. If he only knew that his daughter lost her virginity to an American soldier when she was sixteen. I wasn't that cold. What was she looking for? I wasn't in the moment and I was letting her get away with murder.

Didn't I care?

I was shooting myself every day. Iko demanded more materially than I could give and I was only left wondering if she would not be so dedicated but she was smart and clever and a real cunning immature girl. The more of a bitch she became the greater our sex was. Our love had become an impasse. When we weren't fucking we were fighting.

I was attracted to this aspect of her and so I hid my displeasure. I had become masochistic. We tortured each other. If I ever slighted Iko by flirting with another girl, her hand went into action. I had never laid a hand on her. She was as jealous as I was. I was trying to reason with someone who didn't think, just reacted. I kept wondering why I couldn't slap her but what would that do? I still wanted revenge and I had already missed several opportunities and I couldn't wait for the day when I could get it.

I was looking forward to marriage but now the time we had apart was revealing to me and I had to use it to somehow build myself up for our next encounter. The pressure was growing and growing and I had to produce something soon. Iko had given me a kind of ultimatum. Not to promise anything for the future. I was speechless and my heart sank. She told me to take it positively but how could I? I started to write a book. All this was told to me over the phone while I was trying to write. I could hear her friend in the background laughing a little at my whimpering. What a fool I was and had been. I knew at that point that we had crossed some threshold. I just didn't realize, as always, how stupid I had been. I didn't have to be so possessive but it was a game that I thought I could win.

She knew me all too well and had lost me purposely on the subway in Japan as we passed through Tokyo. I was left alone and lost in a subway car. I sat there alone on the train, wondering if it was finally over, while she sat only a car away smiling to herself. She enjoyed toying with my heart and having me on a string and squeezing the life and masculinity out of me.

I had abandoned her too once in Los Angeles. That argument was some miles from the university and then I left her on the road after dropping off my roommate. He said I should dump a girl like that but he later visited her house. She later called me from my friend's house to tell me she was okay but how did I know that she had done something with him or that I was being played. I was too trusting.

Iko said that I had my chance. I didn't know our relationship could be so simplified. Those games. I had to learn to play the game. I wasn't very good at games but she seemed to thrive on them. I didn't realize it. It was all about cleverness and deception. I didn't have that kind of tact. I wasn't that deceptive with people. It was brutality. The deception left me wide open. Her mother could play mahjong well. We had a practice game but there was never enough time. It was at her house after dinner in Japan. Iko must have learned well from her mother. I didn't have that type of relationship with my parents.

In Japan we traveled only to not be at her home. For everything bad there was something exceptional, almost bordering on fantasy. In the middle there was comfort and security and the thought that it took time to build something and as I neared the train station to her town I exited the train on a guess and I saw her and she motioned to me to join her in the next train car and we were reunited. I was happy but tried to show that I could play this cruel game. Everything I did was wrong and the mountains in Kamakura above her birthplace near the shrines only resonated her aspirations. She was an ambitions woman and she knew it and nothing could stop her desire to get out of Japan. "It won't be too long," I thought I could hear her saying to herself. I was only temporary.

She liked Santa Monica and especially the promenade and expensive handbags but I couldn't buy one and she became highly upset. I could only take notes now and hope that I could buy her the little luxury items that shielded her from the other girls of her stature. Iko needed those material things to protect her from the fierce competition amongst the women of her peer group, who played out class games. Or maybe I just didn't understand women. But I couldn't afford her.

She was a social climber always fighting these little female materialistic battles revealing little tidbits of her envy or jealousy but she wanted comfort all the way down to her bras, of which she bought the most expensive padded kind on occasion. The details and intensity of our relationship grew and so did her sexual creativity. Everything had to be perfect. Her attention to detail only heightened our erotic relationship. Iko put a high price on her sexuality and once after I had gotten my first apartment out of college she came to visit me. We had gone out for dinner and when we returned to my apartment we had sex. She unzipped my pants and pulled out my penis and put it in her mouth. Before that she used to just take my penis out of my pants and play with it. One time she drew a happy face on the tip of my penis. She liked to measure my dick with her thumb and index finger making a circle around my penis and then placing the circle around her wrist. Later she confessed she felt like a sex doll she had seen on a conveyor belt at her hated DHL part-time job, describing its long hair and fair skin.

"I'm not a Dutch wife!" she said on the other end of the phone and hung up.

After shopping at the Santa Monica Mall she would always go to Victoria Secrets. She would spend hours in this store and I was impatient so I waited outside the store. Now I knew why she had spent so much time in there. She bought this purple bra and matching panties and I honestly felt they were for a much older woman. When we finally got home, I saw her bra strap and I wanted her to take off her shirt so I could see her whole bra. Her breasts were sort of small but her padded bra made them appear larger. I took this as a sign of her insecurity. So she removed her shirt. It all matched, the bra and the panties, but she didn't take off her pants, but I wanted to see everything. It all started when she had bent over in my apartment so that I could see the lines of her panties through her pants; she didn't like to show lines but for me she would. She turned a little to look at me to see if I was watching. I had been watching her the whole time. She turned around and smiled and then stood up and came toward me and got on her knees.

She pulled out my penis with her right hand and then placed it in her left hand and motioned me to lean back. She leaned forward and put my penis into her mouth. I couldn't see her face because her hair was in the way. I moved it away from her face but she wanted her hair to hang down so I couldn't watch. She sucked on my penis very slowly, moving her head up and down very gently, and then I came but not before she pulled my penis out of her large mouth.

She would perform oral sex but she had a few conditions and that was that I couldn't put my hands on her head and that she wouldn't wear white. She gave me blowjobs just to pacify me. Maybe just to keep me around. Otherwise she was going to dump me. I'm still wondering how she does this trick with her mouth, sucking really hard pulling her mouth away just in time, making my cum shoot into the air and then she says, "I want a house!"

That was the most expensive blowjob I ever had. She went into the bathroom when she was finished and suddenly reappeared in her new bra and panties and walked toward me. Just when I was about to get up and grab her she rushed into the bathroom and closed the door behind her. My pants were still down. I wanted her again. I just wanted us to love each other and be together and not play sex games. My life was here in America or wherever I'm working and her life was in Japan. She grew up with middle-class dreams of luxury and she didn't want to struggle. I was just temporary, an experience, I thought sometimes. The burden was on me to create a suburban life for her. I couldn't. She was too expensive.

Tokyo

To smooth things over for us in Japan, she whispered in my ear, and asked if I wanted to go to a love hotel. I was at first reluctant to do so but then I agreed. This was her way of calming me down and making things right. I had never been to a love hotel. It was strange, you could listen to any kind of music you wanted and even foreign-language instruction. Some places had a theme or bizarre settings to fulfill your sexual pleasure. After fucking and paying, you received a free ice cream. Everything was supposed to be cool. I let her do this to me, too many times.

I wasn't sure. It was fun.

After returning from Japan I quit my job at the paper and had resigned myself to unemployment, long walks across Los Angeles and Metro Red Line travels, if not by bus. I smoked marijuana at Santa Monica beach and put my feet in the water, where I went to purify myself and rid myself of all my curses.

The long nights on the bus and the poetry that streamed forth from the deepest part of myself fueled my desire to end my loneliness. I thanked my friend Lisa for the poetry inspiration nights but I missed Iko. I couldn't feel more alone and destitute. I thought I had failed somehow but everyone around me thought I was doing so well and that was because I was doing what I wanted to do. I made preparations to become a teacher.

I couldn't afford a car now and I was surrounded by poverty. I was another person with a degree but my spirit was broken. The sun shined through the clouds and I smoked chronic joints on the front stoop with another neighbor of mine before I met Jober. I had rolled a joint earlier and we had smoked it together. We were soon complaining about the management and how things had changed now that the former manager was no longer running the place, Mr. Ko, an elderly Korean guy. I never saw him get mad.

I remember paying my rent for the first time. His apartment was on the first floor. He had a little dog and I knocked on the door. Mr. Ko answered and he invited me into his apartment. I noticed some Japanese books on a shelf in his room. He said that he had lived in Osaka, Japan for a while. It's where he learned Japanese. He asked me if I spoke Japanese and I said no. He lit a cigarette and talked about his former life in international construction. Getting raw materials from different parts of the world and then constructing buildings in Japan. Mr. Ko had been all over the world. I liked him a lot more than the present manager. At least that was something Jober and I could agree on.

I had forgotten about Iko for now. The streets entertained me. I thought back about the Asian homeless woman I had encountered a few days before. I had seen her again recently. It wasn't long ago that I had given her a lighter when a Central American man got my attention and asked me for a light. I had a lighter and she seemed to come out of thin air and I tried to light her cigarette that was half wet and her lipstick was slightly smudged on her upper lip and the sight of her lips gave me an erection. I wanted to run home but I was lost to the streets and the decay. I could feel the sun on my skin but the rest didn't matter at all. What was I going to do? I had no money and felt lost. The pretentiousness of the city had gotten me down. I was in a foreign country now.

I gave the Asian woman the lighter and at that moment I wanted her and my imagination raced at light speed to the end of Sixth Street. Her hair was slightly dreaded like mine. Then came another memory. I thought I was going mad but I had gone mad a long time ago. I was inside a hospital and I was staring out the window. I had lost all hope but then back to the present and Sixth Street and Westlake and the young Asian woman racing in my imagination and maybe I was the one who was lying to myself. I was too busy waiting for the light to change but I wanted the light to stay red forever. I didn't want to cross at all. I just wanted to stay there in that moment. I didn't want to go, but in the end I was left with my thoughts and gave the girl the red lighter and left with my erection and crossed the street, content with my experience but hoping I would see her again. I saw her today talking to a black man but I passed her by wearing my GAP clothes. Things couldn't get any worse.

I am a writer, I told myself, but suffering was part of my anonymity. I wanted fame but for now I wandered down Alvarado Boulevard, past prostitutes and the motel that eroded all morality that existed. I had degenerated like everyone else in my neighborhood.

Last night in the car with Lisa and how she had gotten under my skin, "the world's angriest Puerto Rican–Mexican woman!" That's how I summed up the night exiting her car at La Brea and walking down Hollywood Boulevard. If I could just make her hear me and what I had to say was that I was alive.

My mother had called me the day before and we talked briefly.

"How are you?" she asked.

"I'm okay."

"Do you need any money?" she asked.

"Yes," I said.

I would need money for now and all I could think about

was getting paid. I couldn't even write about my own people. That was left to others who were new to my own culture, which I had somehow abandoned to a world that was sometimes white. I was at a loss or really consumed by my own inept ability to get into print.

How could I get revenge?

March 15, 2000, it didn't matter.

I crossed the street as I could remember and headed home, the thoughts of the Asian homeless woman consuming my thoughts. I passed the crack dealers. Everything was done at a glance and a special look and then the exchange, but I always bought marijuana on Alvarado outside the swap meet at a former theater. It must have been a grand place back in the day.

"¿Tienes Mota?"

McArthur Park was across the street. The fountain shooting water into the sky like cum. I could watch the water all day but time didn't permit me. For now I was still disintegrating.

My former job at the newspaper it was all I could think about and now that I had this time, I had become a recluse. I had no friends and in a matter a minutes they had all crept away from me as if I was cursed or maybe I had driven them away with my self-blame. I was living like a junkie.

My psychoanalyst said that it wasn't my fault and that I should let go and I tried as hard as I could. I could never have the past back. The nightmares I had for weeks and the dreams of Hada and Iko that I had. They spoke to me all the time. Each day I was walking with them and they by my side. That one moment in time that I wanted to journey back to but I couldn't.

Alvarado

Thoughts

Hada had given me my first taste of love and I didn't even know it. I was too hurt and on my way down. She sent me a card when I was in the hospital for depression years ago and that meant the most to me, or was it the phone call she had given me? I thought about her day and night.

I awoke with dreams of my conversation with her by an ice-skating rink and how long had it been since I had been ice-skating. Years, which only compounded the importance of the dream. I could remember her face and the light shining on us and how I told her that "I didn't know so many Persians were ice-skaters." She was silent but I think she spoke. I can't remember her words but the dream was real. I was convinced it was. Then back to her lips again and how close my lips were to hers and our noses almost touching. Then she departed. We didn't kiss and for that reason the moment had more power. All the sex I had with Iko was slowly but surely catching up to that moment but the two moments were no equal to my hallucinating.

I remember when Hada showed our high school history class pictures of her life in Iran. She was wearing her black chador and was cleaning an AK-47 with some other girls. I could see her eyes peeking out or as her face unveiled. The memory had faded but I tried in vain to recapture it, filling in the pieces as much as could. The other pains I blocked out, like failing at sports and making a mockery of myself and becoming a social outcast at school. Hada had rescued me and at that one brief moment, with all of her strength and love, she made me feel whole. My political attitude that I showed in class had almost gotten me kicked out of school but might have made me a hero, when I stood up for her one day in class, confronting a bully. Hada's eyes widened. I didn't know. I was just hurting. How I wanted her now because I was alone and unlovable.

With Iko it was marriage before marriage. I thought that I would be nothing to her without money, and Iko desperately wanted a house and I was under a lot of pressure to buy one for her. If only I could buy her love but this was for sexual pleasure. For Iko everything had a price. She was selfish, nurturing and immature with a woman's lust. The longer I stayed away from her, the stronger my sexual desires became and the more Iko's materialism increased. We were worlds apart but had been brought together by being in the right time and the right place. The summer we met had been good to us but the distance between us was painful. Hundreds of dollars on telephone calls. I couldn't understand why we did it. Maybe I thought for the first time that I had found love. She was cruel but pleasing, supportive but cold.

During my internship at the alternative press I ventured to the Los Angeles County courthouse to watch court cases. Then I was late to my internship but the feeling of being in the courtroom was electrifying to me. I told Iko about my little journeys and Iko's mother soon afterward sent me a care package of Japanese snacks. It was gratifying but I had since resigned to being a writer.

I had been thinking about Hada lately but Iko also, on

my way home from substituting. The walks up Westlake or Alvarado, the streets teeming with people, most of whom lived like roaches on top of each other, but it didn't matter; we all had to coexist, so we turned the other cheek to what was happening around us. The fountain in MacArthur Park still shot water up into the air and I still thought of Hada, day and night. Our dream conversation near the ice-skating rink and our almost kiss.

Hada was my first real taste at love. I thought God had separated us and that kiss she bore for me, how my lips had never really touched hers that day. Now that I had cleared away some memories the experience was fresh in my mind. I had to put myself in the present, but Hada I could never clear from my head. I loved Hada and now I wish I had her in my arms. I was in love then but she didn't know my feelings toward her and I never said, yes. Iko was a woman I both loved and cherished for what she had shown me. Iko had exposed my weakness and revealed what I was, but I really wanted to be respected and taken seriously. She had shown me my shortcomings and had solidified all of my fears, but she believed in me as a writer.

Iko was the daughter of a middle-class Japanese businessman. I could only dream of how he rose to power in his company. Iko's womanly cruelty showed me no mercy. She loved me after crushing me at every turn. Lisa told me that Iko had her own reality and that I didn't understand this phenomenon. It was against my nature but I learned my lesson and suffered the humility of learning about love from Iko. I was stronger now and I thought but it reminded me of crying once as a child after getting oil paints on my pants.

I was walking home again. How my mind could drift.

The sun shined brightly and hurt my eyes. My BCBG glasses were bent back into place after I awoke from the newspaper job's party. I was upset that night and alone and Nora came upon me but I ran from her. She was an aggressive Korean girl from the newspaper where I once worked. I liked her but at that moment I was afraid. I feared Asian women. Iko had made me a little jaded. One of the top editors picked my brain that night and I should have been happy but I was depressed and bitter. She got me a cigarette but then revealed that she didn't smoke and I told her my life story while another writer was grimacing nearby next to an intern who had given me a ride in her 65 Pony car. I was too self-absorbed. I left Iko's brother upstairs to admire the art. I was under surveillance. Whatever I did was going to be reported no doubt. She may have fought with her brother, Kiyo, but they had as close a bond as any brother and sister. We were inside the Gene Autry Western Heritage Museum and we ran out the back entrance through the freshly watered grass but there was nowhere to go. Nora had pursued me all the way outside. I could hear the tapping of her boots behind me and the swaying of her skirt. The water was marshy. Kiyo followed me. I told him to not look back. I turned my head slightly to look back at Nora. I saw her on the edge of the grass with her hands to her sides looking at us as we trudged across the damp grass.

Nora pursued me again at work. Like a panther she moved ever so close to me. It started off as smiles and exposed bra straps tapering on her shoulders. She liked me a lot and was following me around the paper. She burst into the conference room where I was working one day and asked me how much money I made. I thought she was crazy. She sat there as serious as can be looking me in the eye. Her hair was black, pulled back and clasped with a hairpin. Her face started to turn a little red. I got up and left the room. She watched me as I walked out and I closed the door behind me. Her face was pale and oval with high cheekbones. She was Korean, beautiful, smart and mischievous. I forgot about Shonna.

Nora was so voracious and I started seeing her. She had gone to USC, had lived in Japan and Paris and had a rich Belgian fiancé that she had broken up with. She was high maintenance but played it down enough to appear friendly. She lived in Beverly Hills and liked to eat out at expensive restaurants in west Los Angeles. She had wide hips. We smoked pot together at her Beverly Hills cottage. She took me into her room and lay on the bed. Her place looked a little fucked up. I thought it would be cleaner. I thought she would be a little bit more organized. There seemed to be some type of frustration in her life. She concealed it so well. She spoke softly to me like I was a little boy but acted like a pouty little spoiled girl. It was a reassuring voice like a mother would give to her son but sometimes it was the voice of a woman. It felt erotic, arousing. She wanted something but somehow I wasn't responding. The more I ignored her, the more she pursued me. I couldn't resist her in the end and when I gave in, I paid with my wallet. She was everything that Iko was not but just as material. The naughty look she would give you. I was so dumb. She was constantly sending me messages. She became more daring. Putting her hand in my lap in a restaurant and rubbing my leg. I tried as best I could to remain calm and cool but I couldn't help it. Always making me uncomfortable and being amused by my reactions. She waited until I had an erection and then she would stop as if nothing happened. She liked to play with me. She was like a cat with a ball of yarn. She was curious. Sometimes we smoked pot and she would let the smoke drift out of her mouth in sexy sort of way. Then she wanted to kiss. Everything had to be cool. When it wasn't, nothing happened. I kept wondering how I had gotten caught up in all of this. Nora said she wouldn't go past Western Boulevard. I was living downtown and she was from uptown. With her I went to the expensive cafés and restaurants I thought I would never visit. When I paid she rewarded me. When I thought I couldn't meet her material demands she encouraged me.

She was beautiful and voluptuous and for a moment I was happy. I had forgotten about Iko and everything that we had been through. This was now. I had met the present. Nora was exciting and seductive and erotic and nurturing. I had changed during the whole process but I was in transition when we had met and that is the person that Nora had encountered. I kept myself far away and she crept closer and closer. We kissed on La Cienega in the middle of oncoming traffic. I put my hands on her wide ass.

"You like Asian girls, Bernal. I know you do," she said. We were sitting at a café. "I never thought of it that way," I said. "I never intended for it to be this way. They always come after me," I said, wondering if Nora was right. Nora smiled with her eyes as she drank her cup of coffee. It was a smirk, a smile, but again there was the soft-talking woman and the little girl rolled into one.

Nora smiled again. She thought I was Asian and black when she met me. My eyes were noticeably slanted. It got me a lot of second glances from Asian women. The crazy thing about it all was I was as far from Asia as you could possible get. My eyes intrigued Nora besides the fact that she was with a Japanese girl's boyfriend. It excited her that I had dated a Japanese woman and now I was with a Korean woman. Nora was curious about Iko. She wondered about the type of clothes she wore, why she performed oral so much sex, her small bra size and if she liked other sexual positions.

I wondered whether it was really cheating or whether I was falling into another type of relationship, but it felt more like an affair. Two people had come together who had been in long relationships. It was like half-time. Nora was waiting for the game to begin but for now she relaxed on the sidelines. It was subtle. I was surprised at how much had happened. How I had met this Korean girl from USC with a master's degree in English, who spoke three or four languages, whose mother was a painter, father an ex-real-estate tycoon, and whose sister was an actress and lastly a brother who produced Korean pop music. Now I was at the beginning of another fantasy. Why Nora? She had chosen me. She had known other confidants at the paper. She had pursued others but I was a challenge because I didn't give in so easily. I dodged her at times. You could call it cruel but I was trying to be good. Nora was beautiful and smart. Iko was pretty but Nora was much smoother, mature and less insecure.

Nora was ambitious and could write well enough to do Journalism for the Korean Times, in Los Angeles. She had high expectations. I could tell from the black dress, boots and overcoat during winter and the leather gloves on her hands, her red lipstick and brownish tinted hair and oval face. She reminded me of a Korean soap opera star that I had once or twice glanced at while flipping through cable channels. There in the parking lot after kissing me on lips that she used to speak to me like a businesswoman. Earlier in the evening things had a different twist. She wore a white bra and panties under a casual blouse and black skirt. She had invited me over with a strategic phone call. Nora knew that Iko wouldn't wear white so she wore it. Walking into the living room of her small cottage wearing her black boots and white bra and matching panties underneath her clothes, she sat down on a small couch. I entered the cottage but couldn't move. The lights were dim. She called out to me to sit down. I was tired and in a few minutes I had dozed off on the couch. Nora was a little annoyed. Still she called out to me. My eyes opened. I saw her in the distance in the shadows. I got up and walked toward her and then in a small stream of light I could see her hand as it clasped mine and she pulled me toward her as she lay on her bed. We kissed passionately and she fell back. We tossed and turned on the small bed. Nora removed her top but left her shirt and boots on. I thought that it was little strange and lay back on the small bed watching her fiddle with her skirt and adjust her bra.

Nora sat on the edge of the bed and slowly removed her skirt. She stood up and stretched and walked toward the kitchen. I sat up in disbelief. I immediately had an erection. Nora bent down to pick something off the floor but she was only teasing me. I made a move to get up, but Nora was quicker and turned off the remaining lights. She lit a candle and stood at the edge of the bed. I didn't want to move but Nora approached me slowly. I clasped my hands around her waist and slowly moved my hands down her sides while kissing her. She leaned her head back as I kissed her on the neck. Slowly she moved her hands down my stomach, put her hands between my legs feeling only erection, then she pushed me onto the bed but then she sat down in a chair and lit a cigarette and smiled at me in the dark.

"Why?" I asked, a little curious.

Nora just smiled. Her white bra and panties glowed in the dark. Her hips were wide and the fabric seemed like it would give at any minute.

"You like it?" said Nora laughing.

"Why are you playing with me?" I asked smiling.

"Who said I was playing?" said Nora finishing her cigarette.

"Do you really want me?" she asked. "Or do you want her?"

A cool breeze passed through the small cottage. It felt good. Though aroused, I was annoyed by Nora's smoking; at that moment she rose out of her chair, pushed me down and straddled me on the bed. I kissed her on the lips repeatedly. Then she stood up again. I removed my penis from my pants. Nora bent down and blew on it.

We used to meet at Barnes and Noble at Third and La Cienega and have coffee and she would tell me that she wanted it all and that she was thinking of moving to Belgium and would get married, which she eventually did and her parents didn't approve of. The guy had money and she wanted security but she wanted to fuck until she got married. It was all or nothing now. We would smoke out and she would put my hands on her ass. She liked to ask me about Iko and said that Japanese girls could be cruel and they like to play with men's minds. She asked me what my girlfriend didn't like again.

"Did she like anal sex?"

"She liked to perform oral sex," I said correcting her.

"Oh!" she said blowing marijuana smoke into the night air, smiling.

I wrote a bio about her mother who was an artist and she had made a website about her mother to promote her art. She would wait for me sometimes in the lunchroom. She would ease down the sleeves of her shirt so I could see her bra straps and smile and wink at me. I ran away from her at the Christmas party because I was with Iko's brother but also because I was uninterested. We stopped talking for a while and then she called me out of the blue and asked me to come over to her house and we made love.

I sat in her living room a long time before anything happened. Her place looked really messed up. Like she hadn't cleaned it in a while. I thought that maybe something was going on. She had gone in the other room but I wasn't sure what she was doing and I didn't want to make the first move. I was trying to be as patient and unassuming as I could.

"Come here, Bernal," she said in a soft voice.

"Come lie next to me, let's cuddle!"

It was the kind of voice that you thought you would never hear except in kindergarten. It was seductive and cool to my approach. I couldn't really see. The room was dark. I got in the bed with her and then she turned toward me and we started kissing for a long time. She reached her hand down between my legs and started feeling on the erection in my pants. She unzipped my pants and pulled out my penis. She started making it as hard as she could. She got on top of me and pulled out a condom, opened it and told me to put it on. Then she pulled off her panties and straddled me. She kept going up and down and then went slower. She then started pacing herself. She wouldn't stop. Her shirt was open and I could see her breasts. She took off her shirt and bra. She kept moving. We twisted and I was on top of her and then she clutched her legs around my back and I fucked her again. She started moaning but soft. She started to slow down but then I stopped and turned her over and she put her head into the pillow. I kept fucking her. The cellulite on the side of her hips shifted with each movement. I kept going and then we leaned up and I grabbed her breasts. Her nipples were hard. Then she fell down on her hands. She told me to stop but I kept going. Then she put her head back in the pillow. Then she became limp. I stopped and lay back. She turned around and lay between my legs. She slowly reached and pulled the condom off of my penis. She got up on her elbows and started kissing the sides of my penis. She kept doing it until I came. Some of it landed in her hair.

She later moved away to Belgium with her fiancé. She disappeared but I missed her too. Maybe I should have let her know how much I really wanted her but I never did.

A few months before that I was in Beverly Hills, eating at an exclusive Chinese seafood restaurant. Across from me Jodie Foster and Chow Yun-fat. I was calm and cool and ate Mount Blanc for dessert. The girl I slept with from the accounting department was less demure that evening but I only cheated on Iko because she said for us not to promise anything for the future. It had all proved that nothing could destroy my love for Iko despite her attempts to always get away and in the end she would get away and I was getting colder.

The way Iko and I had met, our meeting had been the way I had always wanted it to be and we had both, somehow. So we danced around this moment, and I always planned for the future because she was determined to be a housewife and I was wondering if being a lawyer would create a living that could support her lavish fantasy lifestyle and if our fantasy would come true.

All I could think about was her. How she had crushed me on the phone and how deep down inside I always had this desire for revenge. I couldn't find a way. If only I could have said no to her or maybe walked away or something. Instead I gave her all of the control. I had been alone for months and now that she was going to New York I was crushed. We had become so cruel to each other. She mocked me often. I wanted to reach through the phone and slap her face. Her contempt for me grew. Sometimes it was as if I was never confident unless I was having sex with her. She had to be dominated somehow but at the same time couldn't be dominated by anyone. Iko stayed on my mind. I was degenerating like the weird man that was at the bus that was yelling in the middle of the night as I made it home to my studio apartment with hardwood floors that I was sold on.

Here I am at the present. I should consider myself a loaner and a loser. I was already living on the edge. Just living in my dreams. Tears barely able to come out of my eyes. High on mushrooms. So sad I could crawl underneath a sidewalk. I didn't trust anyone and I don't think anyone respected me in the ideal way that I thought it would happen. It had all become a sham. Nightly I went to the roof to think and clear my mind and sometimes someone was there and we would talk but most of the time

I was alone.

Hada stood still in my mind as always. I could flip back and forth like I was using the remote from a cable clicker. I had to at some time come to the present. I had to snap out of it. I couldn't let Iko get me down like her friend getting ripped off by a fake talent agent in New York City.

It was all fake. I had my brush with fame. I wanted to link it all together. I was still lost in my thoughts. People were concerned but I wanted to stay lost. I had lost my ways and they all warned me not to stray from my path. How long had it taken me to get here? I had become what a friend had reminded me not to become, a Steppenwolf.

I was trying to transcend this period in my life, when I thought I was just going nowhere I could write till dawn. I had risked it all and my education seemed illegal and false and my whole aim at the time I had lost in all my confusion and despair. My head hanging low almost to the ground. That bus rides I had and I thought I was with Hada smiling, the cold San Francisco wind brushing against our cheeks. I was in love, if not for a second and I didn't even know it. I was on the verge. Why couldn't I have been stronger? How much more could I digress? I loved her so. I thought about her constantly and those dreams that I had one morning. I was sure I was there. That moment again when time didn't register anymore. The dreams had taken over my life and I would remain there for the rest of my days. I couldn't trust anything but my dreams and what they left me. Everything became fake, with a thin layer of icing that I didn't like. I had become an illusion to myself and it had cracked me in half. I wanted to be free. Really free but no one would listen to me. I felt totally ignored, anonymous.

"What did I find in Japan?" That's what Jana asked me, my sister's friend, the Union activist and her boyfriend, Peter, the graffiti artist.

I had to return to the party and all the wine I drank to swallow my sorrows and tears and life. The parlor games and salon-like atmosphere of artists and people swallowing wine, time and humor. We could take over the city and in the charades game I played and acted out Jim Kelly, the black exploitation actor and Kung Fu expert.

Jober could be so arrogant that I could ring his neck but maybe it was my own envy for not having something visual besides words spraying out from my mind. The train I rode all day until my mind wandered off into obscurity. This loneliness that I hated ripped apart my mind. I've never felt so sad in my life. So down. The city was falling apart and I had no friends or enemies, just solitude and thinking and worrying about who I was and beginning to despise humanity and myself. Nothing was true and all the homeless men were right in their philosophy and I was insane in trying to believe they weren't telling me the truth. Why was I always wrong and why was I always so lame? I was always wrong about love.

Iko didn't want me to go to Japan. I kept wondering why. She would be working she said and now she is going to New York and why not Los Angeles? And to not see me but maybe it is a chance for her to visit her close high school friends or find a rich American husband. So, I shouldn't worry but I was worried and I always was. I had to control myself. Somewhere I had lost a screw and my mind was totally gone. I might get stuck on Hada's high school kiss on my lips and the short time I spent with her and didn't even know. How lost I was so in my anger and self-pity that I could not recognize something so simple as affection.

Another hallucination after another.

There I was lying on the bottom of the sea. Hidden from sight. Sitting in a mosque, so quiet and how I had lived so deep in sin and against myself when I was looking for answers that where pain couldn't see. My search led me deeper and deeper into my soul and imagination. I couldn't trust myself as far as I could think or do. There my eyes open in the middle of the night. My nightmares, each one getting worse and worse and at Iko's house the nightmare I had and I screamed in the middle of the night enough to wake the dead and not a soul could hear me. How afraid I was afterward? No one to save me but my own will and courage.

I hated walking home alone. On the train I was alone and I felt tired and out of love. I thought about the Ferris wheel in Yokohama looming in the background, the tears almost pouring from my eyes as I walked away from it with Iko. She saying that she couldn't love me in the way that I wanted her to. All my self-worth began crashing into Yokohama Harbor at that moment. I was her slave, moving to her every desire. The bright light bulbs peering from the giant Ferris wheel. The sea air filling my nostrils. Every nerve on my body on end. Her lips pressed up against mine and the intensity I felt. The kiss that I gave her and she didn't seem to mind about the other passengers in our carriage that I forgot about because I didn't care. How we loved each other and rejected each other at the same time. Fucking in a love hotel. She couldn't satisfy me either. I pushed her beyond her sexual limitations but her resistance was part of her game. She always kept an air of ambiguity about herself. That's how she kept control. I wanted her all, every moment. How much could I see? Was I wrong then? She had tortured me all the way down to the end like burning candles. How could she? I was bleeding inside, a thousand arrows piercing me at one time. My heart was broken. I wanted revenge somehow but she was unreachable.

A young couple had exited the Ferris wheel. The girl wore a miniskirt. She bent over while walking with her boyfriend and flashed her white panties. Her boyfriend slapped her butt to cover it up. She turned around and smiled at Iko and me and hurriedly walked away. Yokohama was beautiful and a surprise. It was the first time for both of us. On that trip on the way to Kyoto and Nara we didn't have any sex. There wasn't any privacy. I had little money. The adventure of seeing something totally new for the first time took away these inconveniences. Iko was adventurous. Leaving Japan would be hard and now I understood a part of Iko that I hadn't understood before. My lack of money made things difficult. She joked with a friend once while we passed an expensive store that if I bought her something from that shop, maybe, just maybe I could be her friend.

Trapped in a minute in time. It went by so fast and I was so blind. I was desperate to relive the good times at any cost. I didn't care about anything else. Nothing mattered now. What pieces I could assemble in my mind I would. I would put all the pieces there and relive it again and again. All other past losses would fade into oblivion. I could do this. I could exist alone and write and work and put my thoughts down and not feel like I was wasting my time with love, which only offered me sorrow and discontent. I could only satisfy myself. Nothing else had worked for me. The words crashing from my mind. I tried to pull love from my words but I stood firm no matter what it cost me. It was all I had and I had to put my full confidence behind it. I wanted Iko to have faith in me but I had a dream about her this morning. She was there smiling in the sunlight and it couldn't have been more demented.

Lisa, a Puerto Rican–Mexican girl I had met a few days before, worked with the children that had run away from home and she asked me for my phone number through the bars of the school fence, across where I had taught downtown. The silver hoops in her ears shining like diamonds and rubies. I could imagine her on a pyramid high up in the sky before a ritual Aztec sacrifice. I wanted her and her approach was new and the radiance in her eyes was there. I looked deeper and she smiled, the sun's energy filling us both. There was something pure about her though she was very revolutionary and it was uncommon to see her wearing red and black and her hair put back like in the late twentieth century. These were different times now. An election was upon us, but I wasn't sure if it really mattered.

The parlor games we played and the artists who smiled all the way to the bank. I couldn't have been more crushed. How much wine could I drink or consume? They all thought I had lost it still and when I see my sister and look into her eyes and we stand firm and strong.

We were all that we had. I didn't want to think about it anymore. That Iko was going to New York and I was stuck here or the manager of a movie theater calling me for an interview and how I didn't really want to go at all. I didn't want a job then. I didn't want money but somehow I had to survive this all. I was falling apart but I was trying to remain true to myself. I needed answers but the answers were plain to see. Iko didn't want me in Japan and was against me visiting her at first. What was she trying to hide from me? It didn't matter now that she was gone.

Jober laughed and tried to explain the universe and I think it was all the cocaine we were high on inside the train and I thought back to Mr. Sakamoto who was drunk and tried to organize a barbecue that all resulted in a lot of people and a transvestite showing up to a loft in the arts district off of Traction Street in downtown Los Angles. You just had to go to New York said Pauline and Angela had told me to stop thinking about Iko. I had to believe in myself. I had to write.

PART II

CHAPTER 4

I was looking for something new and different and that's when I met Monique Enriquez. She would call me and leave long sexual messages on my answering machine but I was not interested in her the way she would like me to be, especially after we had protected sex and she later told me that she had herpes.

The sex we had was amazing and it was the first time I had been with someone in long time who enjoyed sex and didn't make me feel guilty about it or who had made sex conditional. It was such a release meeting Monique. I had bent her over and screwed her like a dog. She screamed with pleasure and slapped me on the ass. We were fucking in her grandmother's vintage bed and it creaked like the Titanic before sinking. We were loud and the room smelled heavily of sex. I fucked her repeatedly for hours, taking a small break in between. Her face was glowing like a Christmas tree. She had an ancient Aztec tattoo on her hip that moved as I screwed her. She begged me to cum. I stopped momentarily to catch my breath. She asked me if I wanted a blowjob and so she removed the condom and put my penis in her mouth. Her breasts were pointed and hard because she was aroused. She put my penis in her mouth and started bobbing her head and sucking on my penis, humming and made kind of a slurping sound with her lips. I came in her mouth and she pulled my penis out of her mouth and I could see cum dripping from her lips. She licked her lips like a whore.

After such a fantasy we lay together for hours and then she told me that she had herpes. I didn't know what to do. She said I wouldn't get it because I wore a condom and she wasn't having an outbreak. I told her I felt betrayed, that I could slap her in the face. She then offered to take me home. I told her that I didn't want to go. I immediately felt depressed. She said I could take a shower and I did. I stayed in the shower a long time. Now I didn't want to have sex ever again. She had invited me over to watch *Ocean's Eleven*. It was actually a good film. We had eaten lightly because she was vegetarian. Then we went to her room. Monique was of Mexican and German descent and had grown up in Oregon and she was hotter than the hottest chilies of Mexico. She was fucking gorgeous and fucked the lead guitarist of No Doubt. I had an erection just thinking about her. She left home when she was sixteen and went to New York. She was desperate for cash and so she started stripping in a sex shop near 42nd Street, which now people say looks like Disneyland. She was a peep-show girl. I guy came in and put a dollar or more in a machine, like when you pay your way to ride the subway, and then this slide went up and—bang—there she was nude except for a G-string and high heels. There was a phone where guys could communicate with the stripper. She said sometimes the guys were jerks and wanted her to do more but she didn't have to answer them with her phone. Sometimes the guys would just jack off and splatter cum all over the booth. Women or men would come, young and old. It was a risky job, especially after one of her coworkers was followed home after work and murdered. That freaked her out for a while and it's what eventually led her to quit her job. She wasn't just a stripper but an artist going to an Ivy League art school in New York. Her parents wouldn't pay for her education because she had run away from home. So she paid for it herself and she needed the cash. New York was expensive then, as it is now. She also made extra cash by hiring herself out to private parties and performing sex acts for people, like the octogenarian man, who liked to watch her pee in a cup and then on him while he jacked off. There was more but she wouldn't go into details. Then she met Timothy McDaniels. He came to watch her and toward the end of the show had invited her out for dinner. She accepted. She was a little scared, especially after her coworker had been murdered on her way home. Timothy was an artist and at the time they had met, he was a very unsuccessful commercial artist but then suddenly he started receiving work and became wealthy. He was very unorganized and she took care of that but he was selfish and to make matters worse he had given her herpes and later genital warts, one which was iced off.

Monique had recently moved from New York to California after breaking up with Timothy, whom she'd had a relationship with for ten years. That seemed like a long time to be with someone and not get married and she agreed with my assumption, which is why she broke up with Timothy. Now they were just friends. I couldn't believe they were still friends but she worried about him because he didn't take good care of himself and I believe that deep down inside she still cared about him. You just don't lose that kind of feeling for someone you've been with for that long overnight. I was devastated after hearing her story and also at the possibility that I might have contracted herpes from her. She was a musician. I spent the weekend with her anyway and I went to watch her play the viola at a park in Pasadena near her apartment, which she shared with her sister and another girl, who was there the whole time we were fucking like rabbits. I was looking for something new and I had found it in Monique Enriquez, fresh from New York, tall with slightly reddish-blonde hair and freckles and she liked to dance salsa. She said I was handsome, and I told her I didn't look at myself that way. She said that I was too hard on myself and that I had a nice dick. I think about Monique all the time and about how devastated I was when I thought about her. How I was excited about meeting her because I thought that what I had asked for I had received and that she was someone fresh and someone new. She was a little agitated about my reaction to her having herpes. She said that she had dated other guys and that I was the first to react to her in the way that I did. I quickly reminded her that I was not like other guys and that having herpes was something that I didn't want to deal with and that I had to be honest with myself.

After we had had sex we talked about the future. She wanted to have a family and kids and she didn't want to be too old before attempting it. Then there was the issue of finding someone who would accept her and her herpes. That was the hardest part because they could either react like me or lover her unconditionally. The later was almost impossible. I thought most would react the way I had reacted and that was depressing to ponder. She had caught me in her web and I couldn't get out of it no matter how much I struggled. I was excited about Monique but I was also hurting. It seemed like everything in my life had been that way. That there was always this bad message waiting after the fun was over. Some telegram that I would receive to remind me what type of world I was living in. This was a reality which I had viewed from only a distance and now it was so close.

In the classroom it was the same thing. Nobody cared about anything until it had happened to them. I remember teaching on one assignment and watching how students reacted to theft. A girl who was selling candy left her box of candy in the room. Some students came in that should not have been in the room and they took the box of candy and distributed the candy around the room. The girl came back and said that her candy had been stolen. At first I thought she should not have left the candy in the room unattended. I was angry not only because the girl's candy was stolen but also because I had let some people into the room I had suspected were not students in the classroom. I identified people in the class who had eaten some of the stolen candy and those people became infuriated with me.

I told them that just because the person doesn't know who took their candy doesn't justify the crime. "You don't care because the candy didn't belong to you!" I yelled across the room. I was pissed off. "What if it was your stuff?"

High school students were ruthless and middle school students as well or maybe it was just a sign that our society had once again been transformed. The old rules had changed and I was starting to realize my age. High school for me was both a blessing and a burden. It was a yoke that I did not bare lightly. It hurt as well as challenged me in ways that I was not prepared for. Something in me had been broken inside.

I tried hard to find the answer to my past. It was difficult to move forward when one was entranced deep in thought. It's a magic spell that must be broken. Dreams were sometimes a way to ease one's distaste for reality. It allowed us to bend the rules. Some of us did it more than others. Sometimes you just wondered how you could do all those things in your sleep but it's just a revelation of the mind. That there is a power in us that is beyond our comprehension. Some people realize this at an early age. They live life with so much agility.

Monique came too late, too soon. I told her that if she knew me when I was in high school, she wouldn't have talked with me. She said that she would. It was encouraging. I started wishing that I had met her before she'd met Timothy. Then I could rewrite history and give her life a more favorable ending.

I told her that women were always on this timeline but so were men. That men were on a timeline too and that we also thought about our age and getting married and having children. I thought before she had revealed her painful secret to me that I had finally found someone I could be with. I did but I couldn't lie to myself and be with her while being self-conscious about her having her infection. She said that she had been with a guy before that didn't mind her having herpes. That he had lived in the Bay Area and she had moved up there to be with him and found a job but that he was sexually repressed and had some psychological problems and he couldn't satisfy her.

She didn't want to invest so much time into anyone anymore and then realize that it was a waste of time. It was too painful. She said that having sex with me was the first time in a while that she had had an orgasm and it felt good. The more we talked, the more depressed I became. I started losing heart about having a real relationship with any woman. It just seemed impossible or maybe it was just me. All the sex in the world couldn't make a relationship right but as a human being sex was a part of life. Safe sex was important and I wasn't a fool to think that I could just have sex with whomever with impunity. Everything has a price and I had paid a high price for what I had learned about Monique. I was shattered like terra cotta.

It had been a long weekend. It started off slow before the movie with coffee at a café but ended with a reality check beyond belief. After she brought me home she said that she wanted to remain friends. I agreed because she was a special person to me. I was angry but I pitied her and I was happy that it ended in a positive way but I knew that I had to get tested and stay away from her.

CHAPTER 5

Jober and Johanna had been the first people I had seen after having sex with Monique. I was at a neighbor's apartment when Monique called me to say goodbye to me in the Burger King parking lot next to my apartment. I gave her an old dress I had gotten from my cousin's house near the French Quarter. She stood there looking at me puzzled for a while. "I can wear it for you if you like," she said seductively and kissed me. While kissing me, she reached down with her left hand and unzipped my pants and grabbed my penis. She squatted down and opened her mouth but then suddenly stood up. She squinted, looking into my eyes. I turned to look behind me. Some Latin women who had been inside the Burger King came out to the parking lot gossiping in Spanish and turned their heads towards us when they saw her suddenly stand up with her hand inside my pants. I kissed her again but not before zipping up my pants. Monique took the dress and placed it on the passenger seat of the truck and closed the door. She kissed me one last time and then got in the truck and drove away, leaving me with the dresser she had given me in some sort of weird exchange. She called me the next day but I wouldn't answer the phone.

I felt a few pounds lighter when I had seen Jober's Volkswagen Cabriolet parked at the Burger King parking lot next to my building and rushed off to my neighbor Johanna's apartment on the fourth floor and knocked on the door. Johanna opened and said hello. It smelled like pot. Johanna and Jober had finished smoking pot and were about to smoke again now that I had arrived. Johanna gave a hug and welcomed me in. Jober came and asked me where I had been.

"Sexo con Alemania!" I said to Jober who immediately understood.

"What did he say?" said Johanna who didn't know Spanish.

"Nothing," said Jober smiling."

Johanna had moved from the other side of the apartment to where Jober use to live in 407. It was strange to know that. And before Jober had left he had moved into another apartment 407 before I had left to New Orleans with my mother. Johanna had moved into the building shortly after Jober. Somehow we all met, maybe it was after being at Nate Bob's and playing music for a while in a small little group that quickly disintegrated but not the friendship that was founded. We all liked to get high and Nate Bob had all the drugs we could ever want, especially after Jober and I had lost our connection somehow, but that was later.

Johanna was from Baltimore, fresh from Texas. Her boyfriend was in an indie band and she had broken up with him after living on the road. Now she worked for an independent record label that had made the soundtrack for CQ. It seemed like Johanna knew everyone and had her hands in everything and that could have been because she cut hair. Johanna *was* Silver Lake. She played the part well all the way down to her underwear and vintage clothes and old school Valiant. It was the color of foundation. She had a chihuahua named Je t'aime, a cat called Precious and another cat called Salem. They all somehow lived together. At Johanna's old apartment we smoked a lot of pot, and one night Jober and I had acquired some cocaine. I think Johanna liked Jober and she use to come over to his apartment when we were chilling and she'd be wearing some fuck-me clothes but Jober was on the money and called it like it was and he told me that he wouldn't want to live like Johanna but she was good company and she liked to smoke as much pot as we did. When we weren't at Jober's, we were at her place and that's where I met her friend Susan, another gal from Baltimore. I didn't know Susan well; however, she and I would become such good friends. She was older than me, I didn't know by how much, but I could tell that she was searching for something. Johanna and Susan had been in an alternative band back in Baltimore and had both came out west to support each other in their new territory. Susan worked in the film industry and had been a film major at an art school back East. Now she was struggling to make ends meet. She had light brown hair with a blonde streak near the front. It looked just right and she didn't overdo it with all the vintage crap. She drove an 80s car and she looked better than Johanna.

I had talked with her many times about life and that was at a time that I was reading Krishnamurti and started liking a lot of his metaphysical philosophies and trying to apply them in my life. I discussed some of these philosophies with Susan and she was intrigued by them and she took a liking to me and my mind. I didn't come off desperate like I wanted to get in her pants because she was blonde. She had a boyfriend that she was living with that was wack and Jober and I anxiously wanted to see him. Susan told us all about him and the two looked like Tarzan and Jane. We finally did see Tarzan and I didn't want to stick around to check him out, I only wanted to deal with Susan. The guy drank half a bottle of mescal that Jober had procured from his apartment and passed out and Susan came out and laughed at me and Jober, who had just finished a joint on the balcony. That was a crazy night. Johanna thought things might be heating up between me and Susan and so she always let me know when she was around or coming over and well I had a lot of weed and would smoke them out. One night Jober said that he had been talking with Rambo, the dealer, and he had said that he had some cocaine. So Jober and I met up with Rambo and bought some and came back to the apartment building and went to Johanna's and brought the cocaine. It was my first time doing lines. I had stayed away from the stuff for the longest time. It was also Jober who would do heroin with me. But this night it was cocaine and Johanna's eyes lit up and she produced a mirror that looked like a square tile of linoleum. It was perfect and Jober felt like he was having one of his *Boogie Nights* moments.

"Wow," said Susan sarcastically, "cocaine!"

She was putting on eye makeup in the other room. "Come talk to me," she said. I walked past a wall of vintage clothing to see Susan who was back looking in a mirror that looked like a dressing room mirror with lights all around it. She looked good and she smiled at me when she saw me standing some ways from her. "Come sit here," she said to me. I came and sat opposite her and watched her delicately apply the black substance around her eyes.

"How are you?" I asked her.

"Not too good," she replied. She seemed suspended in animation.

"We got some cocaine!" I said.

Susan turned to me and smiled. She was so white, miles away from me but she was down to earth. She wasn't who she appeared to be. She had broken up with her boyfriend but they were still living together and that was a problem and she had to find a way to move out and not create too much drama. It was not going to be easy. Then there was work because the movie industry could be like subbing and slowing down and now she was applying for unemployment.

I could sense that she was unhappy here in Los Angeles. She came from a wealthy family. The look of longing in her eyes but her grin, she had a beautiful grin. She got up out of her seat and put her hand toward me and I took her hand and Susan led me into the living room. There was a Califone in the corner and Johanna put on a Joy Division record. There were some more old records on a shelf and a giant photo plastered onto a piece of wood that took one whole side of the room and a giant mirror that was slanted against one side of a corner of the wall. Johanna was in the back cutting up the cocaine into little lines.

"Come on, you guys," she yelled at her guests.

Jober was sitting at the edge of a sofa and then he saw Susan leading me by the hand and he smiled.

"I want to go first," said Susan like a little girl. She then went to the back room, passing through beads that covered the entrance. Johanna's apartment was on the fourth floor overlooking Third and Alvarado Street. It was a cool view where you could see the Burger King sign and look down at the cheap motel down below.

Susan had led me in along with her. Susan bent down and put a hundred dollar bill next to a small line of cocaine. She snorted the cocaine slowly up her nose until it was gone. She leaned back upright and smiled.

"It's been such a long time since I've done coke," said Susan walking past me putting her hand on my chin. She waved her head to move her hair out of her eyes and fastened her hair with a clip behind her head. Jober came in then saw me standing there. Susan watched, grinning.

"Come on, dude, you have to try this," he said casually. He told me what do. I bent down and sniffed two small lines of cocaine into each of my nostrils. They tingled a little bit and then I bent back upright.

"How was it?" asked Jober smiling.

"It was good!" I said calmly. It was different.

Soon Johanna was back there too and had taken a hit of coke.

"This is more like diet coke," she said sarcastically. Everyone laughed a little. Jober and I were radiant. Our eyes were lit up like Christmas tree lights and we didn't even know it. Susan and Johanna were silent and smiling.

"Does anyone want anything to drink?" Johanna asked them. "I got some wine, some beer and water."

"I'll have some wine," I said. It's what everyone wanted at that time and Johanna went and got us all glasses of wine. Now we were all really feeling good but Jober wanted to go out and I was feeling a little cagey.

"We're going for a train ride," said Jober all of a

sudden. Johanna and Susan looked at each other. There was big pause for a moment. "Be careful," said Susan looking at me. The two of us stood up and made for the door. Johanna let us out and I looked at Susan who smiled as we left.

"We should take the train to Hollywood!" said Jober. "We should take your video camera!"

Jober stopped by his apartment momentarily and then he got his leather coat, an exact replica of an Indiana Jones coat he had ordered from England for about 300 pounds. It was handmade of brown leather. It was a cold night and he took a pair of blue wool gloves out and put them in the pocket of his coat. He grabbed his knit cap and put it on his head. Then he secured his apartment and went downstairs to my apartment. I was waiting patiently and had gotten my video camcorder and some tape and a battery and put them in my backpack. I put on my beanie and a blue coat. Jober knocked on the door and I let him in.

"Are you ready?" asked Jober.

I was starting to feel the effects of the cocaine kick in. I was feeling alert and pepped up. Jober was smiling. I grabbed my shit and we took off toward the subway. We took one last look at the building that seemed like a castle upon a hill even though it was dwarfed by the massive retirement home beside it. We made our way to the light, crossed the street and headed south down Alvarado.

We entered the subway. It was like a movie set and the light next to the ticket machines seemed brighter. I took my camera out and filmed Jober coming into the subway and paying for his ticket. We got our tickets and made our way back to the lower train platform. The station was deserted. Jober and I started to laugh. It had been a wild night so far. I liked Susan and thought that they all knew it.

So, what!

It just made things interesting. Jober felt the air against his right cheek. He turned his head and looked down the tunnel and saw the light of the train subway train illuminating the train tunnel. The force of the air turned into a small breeze. I turned and looked at the train that slowed to a stop in front of us. We looked at each other and smiled and boarded the train. We were in the end car. I had turned the camera off temporarily but then turned it on again and walked toward the window facing the tunnel. I was filming the reflection in the tunnel and Jober took the camera from me and started filming my reflection in the window. We exited at Hollywood and Vine. It was a November night. A little chilly and there weren't too many people out. Jober and I had found Michael Jackson's star on Hollywood Boulevard and Jober moonwalked across Michael Jackson's star and I filmed it. We burst out into laughter. We also found Woody Woodpecker's star. I was feeling so high and Jober had packed a pipe and he took a hit and passed it to me. We decided to cross the street again. A Middle Eastern woman saw Jober running down the street with the camera. As I approached she looked into my eyes and smiled as if she knew I was on something but the look of silent expression on her face revealed what was on her mind. I smiled back and soon Jober was at my side again. We came upon a group of Scientologists who were having some type of jubilee outside with a band and Santa's North Pole Village facade. But as soon as they saw me with my camera for some reason they fell silent. There was a small crowd watching the show but they could all be Scientologists creating the appearance of a crowd. It looked wacky and I looked at Jober and we continued down Hollywood Boulevard until we had reached the American Cinematheque building. I had turned my camera off and the lady started singing again as we walked away. Some Scientologist tried to hand me some of their propaganda and I waved my hand to shoo them away. Another crowd had gathered in front of the American Cinematheque building that had now been remodeled in Egyptian motif. I had been there sometime after it had been reopened and saw *The Deer Hunter* for the first time on the big screen and the director was there and some of the actors. John Savage was in the audience and he looked back for a second and I recognized him and he turned around. He was with a black woman.

Cameras started flashing and the crowed moved back some and then from within the futuristic, Egyptian, modern movie house came Nicholas Cage. He was wearing an expensive black suit. Bodyguards also flanked him. Looking like Humphrey Bogart, he scanned the crowd but wasn't quick to crack a smile until at some point he relaxed. The autograph seekers surrounded him. I stood at the edge of the crowd filming the whole scene. Jober was less impressed and leaned against a lamp post from a distance, looking at the mob of fans. I caught a shot of him away from the crowd. The actor started moving again and made it to his limousine that appeared out of nowhere like a phantom and got inside with his bodyguards. The crowd followed him to the limousine until it pulled away into traffic. That was cherry. Me and Jober decided that we had had enough excitement and made our way back to the subway station and home. Johanna and Susan would probably be high and talking all night long about Susan's problems or trying to make music.

The ride back to the apartment was a little less intense. I looked at the footage of film I had taken as we rode underneath the city. Jober wanted to see the footage of Nicholas Cage. It was sort of strange and there were even some camera effects put on the image. We laughed because we were so high and wanted to go back home to smoke some more weed. The train got to Westlake and Alvarado. We exited and made our way to street level and had turned to walk up the enormous hill that led all the way to the apartment building.

When we finally reached Johanna's apartment and knocked on the door the two girls looked happy to see us.

"Where did you guys go?" asked Susan curiously, looking at our cheeks made red by the cold night air.

"We went to Hollywood and we saw Nicholas Cage and Bernal filmed him signing autographs," said Jober.

Susan eyes lit up like Baltimore and started laughing and then we all started laughing and Johanna loaded another bowl and we all passed around the pipe and became very stoned. Susan wanted to see the footage of Cage and I hooked up his video camera to Johanna's old black and white television. The image was clear but looked like 7/11 surveillance footage.

"Oh my god . . . that is Nicholas Cage!" exclaimed Susan, her eyes like lights. Then she kissed me on the cheek.

"Yeah we just saw him on the street. He didn't look happy!" said Jober.

Susan was unemployed. She had gotten her own place in Hollywood but had not found a steady job. So, she slowly but surely sold all of her possessions until she just had her car, a few clothes and her cell phone. I had stayed home from work one day and had walked to Echo Park Lake to pick some water lilies to put in my fish tank at home and to feed the ducks some old bread that I had left in the refrigerator. Susan saw me walking with the blossoms. I heard someone call my name and turned around and ran in the middle of traffic and entered her car on the passenger side. She smiled and asked me where I had been and I talked to her about feeding the ducks and picking the lilies for my goldfish back home. She asked whether I would like to visit a church where there was one of the few Wurlitzers that was in existence and a man from French Quebec had come and he was going to be playing. It was the last show for the year. Johanna had taken Jober and now it was time for me to go with Susan. I agreed and she drove me back to my apartment. I exited the car and went to my apartment and put the lilies in the fish tank and grabbed some money.

Susan sat in the car patiently and when I approached the driver's side, I noticed she was wearing a green miniskirt that was slightly polka dot. It looked wild and I had some weed in my pocket and she turned on her car stereo and backed out and drove toward the old Presbyterian church that was built sometime in the early 1920s when Los Angeles was a very different type of city and me and Susan together would have caused a race riot. It was 2001 but that didn't matter, America was still America. We arrived at the church and found a parking spot. It started to rain, and Susan looked at me and told me to hurry and run with her to the church. She exited the car first. The first image to come into my mind was marriage as we entered the medieval-castle-looking church. She took me straight down the middle aisle. Things seemed to be in slow motion. There were drops of sweat on Susan's face. Her blonde hair clung to the sides of her head but seemed to create a perfect shape to the contour of her body. We sat in the front rows. There were other people there sitting in the stiff wooden benches of the church. The organist began immediately after we sat down. The music was eerie but beautiful and resonated throughout the church with its high ceiling and I immediately felt as if I was inside Batman's secret lair. Susan called a friend on her cell phone. I looked at her and asked her what she was doing. She was calling a friend so that he could hear the organist. The music was serious and the audience remained quiet and statue-like. Susan turned off her phone and continued to gaze at the musician, who looked as old as the organ he was playing. I turned and looked at Susan's face. Her cheeks looked so white and a little gaunt. She moved her hand and placed it over mine and clasped it tightly and continued to look at the organ player as he continued to play. Then he stopped and the audience rose to its feet and Susan looked at me and rose to her feet and smiled and then, looking at the old organist, smiled again.

"Do you want to get some tea?" asked Susan looking over at me and I nodded my head in agreement. I led the way out of the aisle and turned and headed for the front door of the church. Susan was beside me. She looked radiant and happy. She leaned over and kissed me. It had stopped raining for a moment but the sky was still gloomy looking but it reminded me of my youth. When I didn't have a care in the world. When I wasn't afraid of waking up and going outside. Every day offered something new and there was something about me that eternally made me feel like a little boy. Walking with Susan was like being in the movie *The Sound of Music*. We walked out into the gloomy morning holding hands. It was before noon. Her car looked like a fish out on dry land. It was a T-top Z car. Susan opened the car doors and let me inside. We sat in the car for a while. Susan put the key in the ignition and stepped on the accelerator. The muffler hummed. It was a cool looking car. We could both remember when cars like it were new. Now it was just kitsch. We drove to a café on Sixth Street and ordered two peppercorn teas. I had never had peppercorn tea but Susan insisted that it was good and she insisted that I try it.

The sky was still overcast and made me feel melancholy. I sat with my tea huddled in my hands. I put on my gray sweater. Susan lit a cigarette sitting next to me. It began to rain lightly, her green miniskirt getting wet. Cars drifted by like ants. I remembered that I had a joint in my pocket and I pulled it out and lit it. It was chronic weed and I passed it to Susan who inhaled it. A waiter from inside the café came outside and told us to put it out. Now we were high. It was a magical day and I hadn't expected it to turn out the way that it had. Susan asked me if I wanted to check out an art show. This was Susan's way of seducing me. I could feel it. It was always the same. I had gotten used to it by now. She kissed me again. That wasn't something that one wanted to be proud of, but Susan was a two-headed key in my hands. She drove me back to my apartment. We hugged and she kissed me suddenly on the lips and I thanked her for taking me out to see the organist and that I would like to see the art show tomorrow.

Susan drove away in her Z car. Her grandfather had a statue in Baltimore for his contribution to firefighting in the city. She was someone prominent. The thought stuck in my mind. She seemed so low but so happy. The next day she arrived like another breeze. It was good to see her again. We took off for an art gallery on Wilshire. We had both been there before. We parked in front of the building. It seemed like everything was taking a long time. We walked side by side and again I looked over at Susan. Her face was beginning to show its age but still looked relatively young and attractive. I liked her and somehow girls just know but this was the easy way. It could have all been a hoax from the beginning, but I had nothing to hide and just admired Susan from a distance as she passed through my life. Her shades were big and round and plastic. We entered through the lobby. An elevator would take us to the second floor where the art gallery was located. A receptionist approached us riding a scooter. It was a quiet place with gay walls. Susan admired a piece of art. I stood back and looked at her again from a distance. It's how I would always remember her. Susan put on some lip balm, the chocolate flavored kind, and said something softly to herself as she looked at the minimalist art. She wanted to kiss. I thought about what she might have said... then she kissed me for a long time.

Now I just wanted to be alone. I didn't trust anyone. I felt like I was still in a Western. The landscape seemed endless and swallowed me up. I could ride the bus to the edge of the city and back. I wasn't afraid anymore. I was in need of a change but I just didn't know what. I wasn't writing like I use to. I felt like the whole world was against me at times and I know that we all felt this way. I believed in providence too much. I thought it was real. I thought about Susan's lips. I thought about Susan buying weed from me in my apartment and how she wrote me a check and did it while sitting in a fetal like position. I wanted her then. She looked sexy and arousing. I wanted to fuck her. At Taix she bought me a drink and the Argentinean bartender spoke to her in Italian and called her a beautiful baby girl. We had eaten Mexican food before that. It all seemed like a dream.

My apartment where I slept and worried and departed from to ride the subway train in vain and sometimes the bus. I didn't speak unless I was spoken to. I never felt like such a loaner. I didn't really trust anyone and I was somehow unable to really socialize at all. I really couldn't. I was left to my thoughts all the time. I was so quiet that people had to provoke a conversation from me. I didn't like things to be this way. I lived downtown. I was poor. I wanted to remain inconspicuous but I stood out. I really did. I could speak a little bit of the city's language but everything else seemed like bullshit.

Back to reality.

After seeing Monique, the next day after she had brought me home, I started calling clinics to see where I could get tested. I was really worried about getting that shit. I didn't want it and she seemed to take it so casually. I felt inside that I had a right to feel any way I wanted to. The way we met. Monique would never leave my thoughts. Just seeing her there in the sunlight amongst a crowd of people. How beautiful she had looked to me. I didn't want the tape to roll forward anymore. Then she did come and talk to me. It was really unexpected. Anything was possible. It was. There on her arm with its other tattoo. I was really afraid.

I walked downtown to a county facility. I arrived a little bit early but I wanted around until twelve when it opened and went and bought a newspaper. It was a hot day. I was wearing shorts. I hadn't been able to sleep. I had to know for sure that I wasn't' infected. I thought there was a test for herpes but there wasn't. The only way one can know is when they show signs of an infection, an open sore. I signed my name. The receptionist was supposed to give people numbers, but he called people by their first name. It was sort of strange. He rattled on with some black girl who had just walked in. They both gossiped about becoming correctional officers. The rest of the people were Spanish speaking except for two college-aged preppy white kids. They had a cell phone but no insurance. I thought they would have health insurance but they looked like they were out of place. They mocked the receptionist. I tried to keep cool by reading a newspaper. My number was one. The male nurse opened a door and called out "Numero Uno." I had a lot of questions. I just wanted know if I had it. I tried to think about how I would answer all of the questions from the doctor or what I would tell the nurse.

A Filipina nurse interviewed me and asked me to fill out a questionnaire. She asked me if me had been out of the country. I told her that I had been to Cali, Colombia. Then she started asking me about tanzine and omerite, all of these different kinds of gems and stones that I knew nothing about. "Where's your birth stone?" she asked me.

"I'm not a jeweler," I said indignantly.

The nurse gave me some pamphlets, winked and sent me out of the room to wait until I could see the doctor. It was back to the crummy lobby again. There were about fifteen people in the room. A lot of people were reading. For some reason I wanted to laugh. There was a mestizo woman with kids in the waiting room. All that was missing was an ice-cream man and a garbage man. The receptionist was irritating but funny. After seeing my dreadlocks, he immediately started talking about chronic weed with another waiting client.

A half hour later my number was called again.

"See doc I had sex with this girl but I wore a condom. Then she tells me she had herpes. She performed oral sex on me."

"When did you have sex with her?" asked the Chinese doctor.

"About a week ago," I said, looking down at the floor.

"There is no blood test for herpes and the only way to know you have it is to show symptoms," he said rather concerned.

I knew there was no cure for herpes. I told the doctor thanks after he looked at my dick and determined that it was okay. It felt good to be out of the hospital but still I felt this lingering worry that there was a possibility that I had the virus. It was making his stomach turn but I knew that I was going to be okay.

Fuck ... the past...

Hada's brother had fought in the Iran and Iraq war and had gone mad on the battlefield. She told me this, the one piece in the link that I could barely remember. I had become him. I didn't know where he was and I didn't ask. Women were so strong and I had been so weak. Hada was so smart and had taken classes at a junior college, studying chemistry. I think I can recall she had aced them all.

Institutionalized...

Brilliant, I thought, and me, what could I do? Nothing! Just read and read and the words coming out of me that I scribbled down into my diary. My hospital mates were mostly rich kids all in here for taking too much LSD from Telegraph Avenue in Berkeley, suicidal teenagers from the suburbs or my best friend, a drug dealer from Oakland, who wouldn't take his insulin. I fought all the way to the end. As much as I could. I just stared out at the walls out the window onto the street and ate hamburgers and occasionally took antidepressant pills and sometimes I had to draw a picture and see a psychiatrist and I had blocked Hada out of my brain when I should have tried to explore and see what she had to offer. Like water she was at that time. So close to it I didn't want to drink but when it was far I desired it more and more.

I would do anything to get back to that time in my life. And should I write off Iko? Should I just let her drift away from me? Should I let her go? I felt that I had really lost her. She let go first and I would somehow never see her again. That's when I heard her voice last, I didn't think that would be the last time that we would talk ever again. I knew she was gone from the day that we met.

From the beginning it looked like love but it wasn't, it was lust. What did I expect? Things had happened so fast and I wondered if it was true. Now I was crushed and let down. I guess it was supposed to be different but it wasn't. I had met someone who could devour me whole and not even flinch and who was silent and quick, but she was honest.

How long had I been held down here on this trip? My whole life fading away into my dreams. I was never satisfied and my dissatisfaction had destroyed all of my dreams and intentions. Somehow my heart just felt like it had broken in two. All the pressure was on me. Why should I care about a person who had no dreams about a future with me? It's what my psychoanalyst had asked me one session. I had repressed so much over time that I missed the simplest things. I opened the gate at the bottom of my apartment and let myself in. I walked up the stairs. I was welcoming myself to the end. The loneliness that I felt killed me in every way. I would never be the same again. I would never love anyone the same way again. Love had ruined me. I ran away from it before and when I finally said yes I was stung like a bee and it hurt. Would it be my turn again? Would I be let loose and let go? Would I be crushed all the way? I thought about my first college editor too, not the wicked one. How I saw her in the rain one day and the way that it made me feel and her eyelashes were wet and her soft voice and she came to me for answers and in the end I let myself go and confessed to her my attraction to her and made a fool of myself and felt ashamed. I had betrayed her trust and I could never go back. I wanted to repent but it was too late. I had gone too far. Then she was replaced by the witch. I got fired from my university college newspaper columnist position but I had won a prestigious student journalism award. At that time I thought that was all there was. I was so alone. Amanda didn't understand how desperate I was but she couldn't wait for me either and floated away like a feather.

I had found a love of writing but what did it mean now? Love so far away was not real. I was dreaming. I felt down. So down. I could sink. I wanted to keep myself pure but I was failing at it, miserably. I could just cut off contact with the outside world and not even care. I could do that. It was like life didn't matter anymore. Where had I met such solitude before? This wasn't the first time that this had happened to me. I felt really alone and lost but I had made it through those times by writing and now here I am again feeling the same way. I was going nowhere and I could repeat those words to myself again and again. Time had slipped past and I was struggling with it and I thought I was getting better and better and not worse and worse. I think that I was starting to see that Iko and I could never get married and that maybe she was only being as honest as she could with me. Would I write sad stories and put them on the internet? I was trying my hardest not to. I could stay up all night and write and who would listen to me? I couldn't go any deeper down and the brother I saw on the bus dressed like an angel of war, who said I was too spiritual and that I should change my name. I followed him some way with my eyes after he departed the bus and disappeared into the city. So there was good that was out there. There were things that I could read about and understand that might make this picture clearer. They were all drawn to me and I didn't have enough time to wonder why.

I sat in my apartment and drank red wine and lit a joint and then maybe I would compose a letter to Iko and then I would tear it apart and contemplate if I should have mailed it to her. So all these letters are just siting around here collecting dust and piled up on the floor. Maybe I was lucky enough to throw some of them away but I held onto them for good measure. But I couldn't forget my love. It wouldn't fade away. Now in my own strange way I was coming to terms with the past. Just me and my words and my small existence and what did it mean and the moment was gone. I was sincere when I was high on mushrooms. I was really trying my best to be sincere. I hadn't known such pain till now. I had let go of my anxieties and now this gush of emotion that was so strong had taken me over and was overwhelming. It had been locked away inside of my brain in a drawer of thoughts for so long. Writing and books provided a relief and became my salvation. If I didn't write I would die. I forgot about it all for a moment and then realized that I was really alone and different from everyone around me. I am a writer. For now my heart was ripped out of its self. I was alone again and wanted to escape. I thought there was nothing here for me. I needed something more but I could only think about Iko.

Here I was.

So close to the end but my thoughts of her spurned me on and that is what I really wanted. I had to keep writing.

Had it all been a fetish?

I think and maybe it was her erotic nature but it was also real and we shared something strong. I held onto our discarded pieces of love. I held onto her hand and she held onto mine. How much had become a fantasy for me though? Did she know and was she treating me the same way? But she was cool to me. She tried to love me. I could only wonder and the things we knew so deep and dark about one another. So we loved and fell out of love and departed from airports and argued over long distances.

I didn't know.

She just wanted to escape but it was easy because in the end she had somewhere to go to and in the end I didn't and it was the source of all my frustration. I kept her in my mind but writing kept the peace. In my dreams my loves were vying for my affection but only one was really pure and would always be pure and that was the balance. Each love looking the same in my waking dreams. I awoke each morning with a smile and dreams of Iko or sometimes of my desires. Each passion had become a manifestation of one or the other. It was only now that I found myself wrestling with these ideas. Maybe I was just hallucinating too much.

My mother had kissed me on the forehead the other night and a part of me was reluctant to have me near her. We had just returned from New Orleans. I felt so ashamed of that, that feeling and my aunt gave me twenty-six dollars, in church mass and the fiery African-American priest, an uncle, telling me to keep on holding it down and have faith in God, and I was trying my best to do so.

I could listen to music all day on the Santa Monica Promenade or Venice Beach or Congo Square in New Orleans and stare at tourists while looking possessed and un-materialistic. I could look amazed and happy and startled and excited but I would only be lying to myself. I was lost. There was nothing that could break the spell. A dark hunger enveloped me and kept me forever locked in its teeth. I wanted to let go but I was stuck. My mind trapped forever on rewind. I wanted to escape. I pushed myself to the end all the way. I could sleep for weeks without leaving my apartment. I had to get out at some time and explore and not let all of this shit get me down. That's when I encountered the writer Andrei Codrescu coming out of the subway at the Westlake Red Line Station. He said to keep to the Eastern philosophies of India, jokingly asking if Lamar Alexander would win the Democratic nomination. We exchanged some information but it dawned on me years later whom fate had allowed me to encounter. A great writer and poet from Romania based now in New Orleans, Louisiana. He was like an angel that came out of a subterranean tunnel. A voice I was to heed. The list of novels he gave me and an email that is now lost when I had finished my reading list. I wanted to rise above my sorrow but I couldn't. I was stuck. I felt like I was going insane. I had never been so alone in my life. I really wanted to find myself and my writing. I watched the writer walking back into the metro tunnel. It was a sign. I had my writing and was in touch with it but would I let Iko go or let her consume my soul?

CHAPTER 6

Mrs. Veracruz was doing well but dealing with her past bankruptcy and now our meetings had become less frequent but all the advice she had heaped on me before. She was my spiritual guide but who could save the old Cuban exile and me, not her Moroccan blood boiling and her keen sense of self and life and me listening for any clue that might help me but I was at a loss. I was trying to turn silver into gold and gold into diamonds but It was a long process.

I had to see her. It was my ritual. We liked to drink Cuban coffees and gossip about our lives. That's how we learned about each other. Our birthdays were on the same day. There were so many parallels in our lives that it made our relationship sort of supernatural. I liked that. I only wish sometimes she was my age but I'm comfortable around women. It depends who it is of course. Maybe it's just a part of my growing up and being around a lot of women while my dad was astray.

Mrs. Veracruz noticed that I was always in this melancholy state. Now that Iko was gone she could see that I had been cut in half. She had her relationship problems but she wasn't alone. There was nothing worse than being alone. These times when I craved it but I think that being with someone is a whole lot better than being by oneself. Some people just make it look so easy and I wonder how they do it. There are people in this city that are so poor but they have each other and then there are people with so much that they can't find any of the answers to life. I didn't know what to think about relationships anymore, especially after being with Monique. I felt really depressed about meeting women. It just seemed impossible. I knew that I could do it but it just seemed like it was over my head. My dad said I was too picky but I think it was that I was operating on a mixed economy. That's the only way that I could put it into words. I needed something new I kept telling myself. I needed something new.

Everything that I had been taught about women was wrong; life was much more real than some textbook. All you could really do was be prepared with your own response to the problems.

Dodging traffic I came to the bottom gate of my apartment. It felt good to be home, regardless of the fact that it was my new prison.

The nightmares had stopped for me now and I was getting regular sleep. Between day and night, that is when I usually awoke. Just in time to see the sun casting light on the world. All anyone could do at this time was make a wish and hope that their dreams would come true. I could hear myself now, screaming in the middle of the night. A couple of times I had awakened my neighbors.

What had I said?

It didn't matter.

They all thought I was mad and I didn't care. Life was fleeing me.

My apartment was more like a coffin of books, papers and magazines.

The sunlight shined through my apartment windows and into my eyes every morning. I forgot about my nightmares. I didn't want to remember them and so they became visions. A moment in the night when I wanted to journey back into Hada's arms, but I couldn't. She was gone and had left me all alone, to my dreams. The conflict between past and present was turning the vivid dreams into fears. The nightmares came from trying to remember her face. She had kissed me once, so I thought, and at that moment, the event became frozen forever in my mind.

How does a girl disappear with her kiss still on my lips?

Not in San Francisco, which is where we were in the plaza, outside of San Francisco City Hall. It was windy. She called to me and I turned around and found her lips. They were soft. The world stopped, and the concrete and marble around us vanished. It was only a second, less than a minute and I had never left the encounter.

I was still in love with her heart at that moment. The remembrance of our first kiss was becoming sweeter and sweeter until I came to the core of it, but there was nothing left to chew on now except the pause in Hada's gaze. It would mark her final meeting with me. Her mother wore dark tinted Gucci sunglasses and was looking at me through the window of her BMW, as I stood silently in a Mervyn's department store parking lot, next to Hada, in Hayward, wondering what to say to her mother. It's how I had last remembered her. She had been a computer science major at the University of Tehran. Her degree was worthless here in America. Only Hada knew how much frustration the situation had caused her mother. The arguments Hada had with her family would last all night long. So she fled to San Francisco, taking the BART train. The kiss she had given me remained in my mind forever. It had the taste of green apple, sweet but sour. Hada had chosen the lip gloss, just for the occasion. I was paralyzed by Hada's gesture but then Hada pulled away from me abruptly after the kiss. It all happened so quickly. I didn't want to remove a piece of Hada's hair that was in my mouth, stuck between my red lips. I could taste her. She pulled the strand of her hair from between my lips and smiled.

I could still remember the pictures of Iran Hada brought to our high school history class. The one photo of Hada body covered in her traditional clothing, except for her face. Only her nose, which protruded somewhat in the middle, could be seen. The smile on her face in the photo could barely conceal the fact that she was holding an AK-47. It was the height of the Iran and Iraq war. Her brother had been drafted into the war and lost his mind on the battlefield. For some reason I reminded Hada of her brother. It's what brought us together. I had replaced the only man she had really been close to. Her father died when she was three.

I had almost ruined the kiss, but she held her lips tightly to mine, long enough to let me know she liked me. Her lips didn't really seem to be touching mine, maybe they didn't. Books came after the kiss. She had remembered that my mind was like a sponge. Our love grew little by little, like loading the magazine of a machine gun. But now the memory of that kiss in San Francisco was fading in and out of my mind. I didn't know where she was. That was the most painful part, waking up from the nightmares.

PART III

CHAPTER 7

Before

A Sourpatch candy wrapper lies on the back seat of the Ford Taurus station wagon driven by Asad Nassir. There were still two more pieces of candy left inside the package for someone to eat. It was dawn. I was getting sleepy now. Yesterday Asad had dragged me to the Key Club.

"What are you doing?" asked Asad.

"Listening to music," I said.

"We're going to the Key Club. Do you want to join us?"

"What kind of music?" I asked Asad.

"Trance . . . we're just going to have a little fun."

"Alright," I said.

"Dress casually," said Asad.

"Okay."

"Do you have any weed?"

"No," I said.

"Can you get some?" Asad asked.

"I think those guys might be out there," I said a little hesitantly.

"I'll come pick you up at eleven."

"Alright."

I hung up the phone. It was quiet now. I had to go on the street. It didn't take long. Asad came at eleven. I was waiting on the steps. I saw the brown station wagon pass by my apartment and then begin making a U-turn. Asad looked relaxed. He was wearing a black silk shirt, tan pants and black shoes.

"Where are they?" asked Asad.

I pointed and Asad drove. Awad was with him and extended his hand to me.

"How are you?" asked Awad.

"I'm alright." I said.

Awad appeared different to me this time. Now he looked hipper. It was only a month ago when I had seen him reading the Koran. The next day they went to the mosque and I had almost converted to Islam. The imam was patient and Asad had arranged a meeting for him and me.

In the basement of the mosque was the washing room where people could cleanse themselves, before prayer, according to Islamic law. Asad washed behind his ears, face and feet and instructed me to do the same without looking conspicuous. The imam was already aware of me. The holy man's presence echoed like the ripples of a pebble thrown into a lake. Their meeting was simplistic and short. One dream had ended and another began. Arabic sounded like poetry to my ears. It was the beauty of the language that struck me. Awad said Lebanese women were the most beautiful women in the world.

Awad's sunglasses were tinted yellow. He could have been sleeping but he was quietly gazing out the car window. I looked into his eyes. Awad seemed so peaceful and calm. But what was he really thinking about? Now Awad seemed like a new person or maybe he had always been the same person. He was wearing black slacks and a creamed colored short sleeve shirt with a black dragon pattern on the back. Awad took out a package of Marlboro Lights and pulled two cigarettes out of the carton. He offered one to me. I took the cigarette and placed it in my mouth. Asad took out a lighter from his front shirt pocket and lit his cigarette and then lit mine.

"Alakim salam?" asked Awad.

"Salam alakim," I said, inhaling smoke from the cigarette.

"Are you still writing?" Asad asked me while looking out the passenger side window of the station wagon.

"Yeah, but things are moving slow now. I'm not at the newspaper anymore, so I don't have an audience for my work, except myself," I said sheepishly.

"You must be lonely," said Asad, taking a drag from the cigarette and still staring out the window.

"How did you know?" I asked curiously.

"I can just tell," said Asad, in his soft-spoken Egyptian voice. Asad read me like a book. I didn't know my look of loneliness was so obvious to everyone. Awad then turned to Asad and said something to him in Arabic. I reclined in his seat. I hadn't realized how I had appeared to everyone, that my loneliness and longing was exposed to the world.

Asad and Awad had come from Cairo. Awad was studying to become an auto mechanic. His father was the owner of an import export company. Asad was studying economics at USC and his father sold electrical supplies. A lot of them coming into contact with these two strangers from Cairo was another mystery of his life. But Asad and

Awad's home, Cairo, was just another faraway place I had never been to.

"Do you see them?" asked Asad. They were looking for the marijuana sellers near Alvarado and Sixth.

"I see them, " I said pulling into the parking lot of this Mexican restaurant.

Asad did as I had instructed.

"How much do you want?" I asked.

"Just get twenty-five bucks," said Asad.

"Okay . . . I'll pay for it," I said.

I opened the back door of the Taurus and slammed it shut. I ran across Sixth Street toward the stairway of a strip mall. At the top of the stairs was an open metal gate.

"¿Tienes mota?" I asked the drug dealer in Spanish. The short mestizo man was sitting against the wall drinking a forty-ounce bottle of malt liquor next to some other men, who were squatting in a small circle.

"¿Cuanto questa?" asked the man as he got up and walked towards me.

"Veinticinco dollares," I said.

The mestizo man pulled a small plastic sack of weed out of his pocket and waited for me to hand him the money. The whole exchange took only a few seconds. When it was over, I put the small plastic baggy of weed in my pocket and ran down the stairs and across the street to the station wagon.

"Did you get the weed?" asked Asad.

"Yeah!" I said, glad to be safely back inside the car.

Asad started up the car, backed the car out of the parking space and drove back toward Alvarado and turned left.

I had never been to the Key Club and he got in for free,

the first night I went. The club consisted of three levels, including the basement that had a bar and a DJ spinning hip-hop. The middle level consisted of a stage area, with a bar, surrounded by standing isles. On the third level there was another bar and chairs and stools. The cover was five dollars. Ecstasy was thirty. Trance music was booming inside the Key Club and the place was packed with people. DJ Bobafet was stoned on coke, playing trance music, high above in a DJ booth, pulled up above the ground, on a small stage suspended by steel chains. It wasn't my kind of music. It was cheesy. I could see him from the dance floor. I spun around for a better look. It reminded me of the nightmare I had that morning. This dream wouldn't end. Nothing was real. I had to keep dancing to keep the allusion going. Soon it would all be over. Between dawn and dusk I survived my nightmares, now I was with the Arabs and DJ Bobafet, who was high on cocaine from Cuba.

"Are you having fun?" asked Asad. He had taken an ecstasy tablet earlier. Now his whole world was a whirl of spinning lights. His body moved to the tempo of the music as it slowed down and then sped up again.

"Yeah," I said lying.

A white girl with red hair began to dance next to him. She looked at me for a long time.

"This is Jennifer," said Asad to me.

"Hi," I said.

"Hello," said the girl.

"Where are you from?" I asked her, after noticing her accent. She could barely here him over the loud music blaring from the speakers.

"Scotland," said Jennifer, speaking into my ear.

She then spun around toward the center of the dance floor near Asad and started dancing with him. She motioned with her hand for me to follow her. I moved toward them and they formed a small circle. Suddenly they were surrounded by a group of people. It was a mixed crowd. I stood out.

"Are you on ecstasy?" Jennifer asked, speaking into my left ear.

"Pot!" I said looking into Jennifer's eyes.

I had never taken the drug and didn't want to. Asad was always trying to get me to try it, just once. He told me said that I would never be the same againc and that I could really understand the music better if I would take ecstasy. I was sure that I could hear the music better if I was on ecstasy, even the details in the electronic music that Asad loved so much. He was sure I would hear everything and that the sensations would be beyond anything that I had ever felt but I didn't think I had to go any further with drugs. Weed had always been enough for me but it seemed that everyone was on ecstasy and loving it.

"What are you on?" I asked Jennifer. She smiled and spun around again then came towards me and spoke into my ear, once more.

"Ecstasy," she said, smiling. Her jeans seemed too tight and her red shirt seemed to glow. She looked much older now, maybe thirty. Awad was nearby and when he noticed I was coming near the group and he smiled.

"I come here all the time alone," Awad said to me in his soft Egyptian voice again. Though he was soft-spoken and the music was loud, for some reason I could hear every word Awad was saying.

"Sometimes I come here alone," Awad said again. I had

heard him the first time.

I smiled back toward Awad, who then put his hands over his head and walked over behind a girl near him and started dancing behind her. The girl was actually a woman and she didn't mind Awad being so close to her. Awad made things look so easy.

Could it be the ecstasy?

I didn't know what to say but should I say anything?

I didn't have to.

The whole scene reminded me of a cheap movie. The surreal visions of Hada had sifted from my mind. Now I was in some strange club, listening to music I didn't particularly like and the people around me had changed into completely different beings. The high from the joint I had smoked earlier had faded but the euphoria of the ecstasy takers was just beginning to kick in. All of a sudden everyone began to focus their attention toward the stage as two women appeared at either end of the stage. They wore bikini tops and G-string bottoms and devil masks on their faces, and they began to dance wildly to the beat of the trance music. The crowd surged with energy and people started to scream and dance more wildly. The show had just begun. A large movie screen was suspended high above the dance floor. The image of a Tabby cat was projected onto the screen. On the left and right of the large screen were smaller screens, the material of the screen slightly twisted. The space shuttle could be seen taking off on one screen and the picture of a beautiful model on another. The images intersected, superimposing themselves onto the walking Tabby cat. Lights of various colors flashed throughout the club. The music changed again and new dancers appeared on the stage, and a new

DJ was inside the DJ booth. I didn't know what to make of any of it. I had never experienced anything like this before.

"Crazy huh?" said Asad, elbowing me.

"Yeah," I said, staring at the dancers on the stage. The dancers danced rhythmically to the music catching every beat, even when the music slowed down, fluctuations in the tempo the music only seemed to make the crowd more hyped.

"Can you feel it, Bernal?" Asad asked me. He was still dancing with the same woman.

"Yeah," I said in a low murmur.

The two masked bikinied dancers left the stage underneath the DJ booth and new dancers appeared. The new dancers were even more daring. A man in a top hat and cape and bikinied briefs stood side by side with a woman wearing a black bra and panties. The lady bent over and faced toward the crowd. The attention of the crowd shifted to the stage again and the trance music became more intense. Her bearded accomplice who looked more like a magician from a low budget porno film, moved his cape back slightly with his left hand and reached behind him and brought forth a pitcher of chocolate syrup. He began to pat the women's behind and started to pour chocolate syrup over her butt. The woman gyrated her body as the dark liquid oozed down the center of her ass. She then turned toward the club and her partner continued pouring the chocolate syrup down the center of her body over her breasts, as she used her hands to baste herself in the chocolate goo. The syrupy woman then took her index finger and scooped a small finger-full onto her finger and placed into her mouth. The crowd roared, forming a type of echo that felt like a wave of sound. I looked into Awad's eyes and could see his dilated pupils beneath the yellow-tinted lenses of his sunglasses.

Only Jennifer, Asad, Awad and I had come to the after party. The drive from the Key Club to the after party didn't take long. It was held at George Gemini's house, and was sometimes attended by young suburban white girls who liked ecstasy and cocaine. George Gemini organized and ran the spectacle that I had seen earlier. Everyone had left the club, as soon as the light came on. They drove farther west, their tired occupants coming down from an ecstasy high.

George Gemini played the role well. He had graduated from the USC School of Business at the top of his class, on a student visa from Burma. A small import-export business he had started failed to materialize. He held parties at his west Los Angeles apartment and then realized that he always surrounded by beautiful people. Becoming a club promoter seemed like a quick way to make money and mingle with the young and the rich from USC. The elite crowd that had money to burn and who were looking for a good time and good drugs. George Gemini had filled a void in their lives.

George Gemini loved to tell the story of how one night a tall blonde girl had looked for him all night, during one of his shows. She kept asking everyone where he was until she found him backstage and gave him a blowjob and left him with his pants down. Awad sat next to me on the couch.

DJ Bobafet was really named Ahmed and was George Gemini's brother. Their cousin, a big-time drug dealer, named Ahmed—after the prophet, DJ'd during the second half of the strip segment of the club. All three of them were from Burma. Ahmed was excited. It was the first time he had DJ'd one of his brother's shows. I was taking it all in, as he sat on the couch of George Gemini's three-bedroom, two-story townhouse apartment.

"How did I do?" Ahmed asked everyone. He was a little jittery from all the coke he did during his DJ routine.

"You did good, man!" said Asad smiling.

"Did you like the dancers, Bernal?" Ahmed asked me.

"They were interesting," I said, still recovering from what I had seen at the Key Club.

"Would anyone like some coke?" George Gemini asked everyone in his thick Burmese accent.

"Sure!" said Asad laughing.

Everyone began to laugh, even me. Couches outlined the table where the small group sat. George Gemini had pulled a small baggy of cocaine from underneath a large glass coffee table that the couches surrounded. He then began to pour some cocaine onto a huge glass mirror that was also lying underneath the table and began to cut up the small mound of cocaine into several lines to snort.

"It was so funny," Jennifer began to say.

"I went to the doctor for a checkup . . . my doctor asked me to breathe during the last part of the physical. I guess he didn't like what he heard because he said it sounded like I had some blockage in one of my nostrils."

Jennifer started laughing loudly and soon everyone was laughing. Even me. The joke made me forget about Hada and nightmares. Jennifer bent her body toward one of the five lines of coke that Gemini had made. She took a hundred dollar bill she had rolled up earlier and placed over the line of coke and sniffed the white powder up her nose. Everyone but me snorted a line of the cocaine.

"Don't you want any coke?" Ahmed asked me.

"No," I said staring at Ahmed. A little white residue from the cocaine was stuck underneath Ahmed's left nostril.

"You have to try this man. This is caviar . . . do you know what caviar is?" Ahmed asked me.

"Fish eggs!" I blurted out.

Everyone laughed.

"No!" said Ahmed.

"Caviar is premium coke man. You know when they boil the coca leaves in water, a cream rises to the top of the boiling coca and this cream is very pure and potent. It's the best part of the coke to use before they cut it."

I listened intensely to Ahmed's words. George Gemini began to giggle but kept his composure. Everyone else stared at me and smiled.

"This is the best kind of coke. It's so pure. It costs three hundred a gram," said Ahmed, bending down to snort another line of Caviar cocaine.

Jennifer laughed.

"That would be telling, wouldn't it!" Asad said, smiling at me.

It was 5 a.m. Asad and Awad bought some caviar cocaine and a burned CD of trance music from Europe and then left the after party. The night seemed to have ended as soon as it began. The Ford Taurus station wagon edged east along the Santa Monica 10 Freeway.

I sat parallel on the back seat of the station wagon. Awad asked me for the small package of the weed he had scored earlier. I gave it to Asad, who poured a small amount of weed onto a CD cover, lying on his lap. Then he poured a little of the caviar cocaine onto the weed. Asad mixed the weed and the cocaine together carefully and rolled the concoction in a white Zig Zag paper. He put a filter on the baseball-bat-shaped joint. Asad told everyone to roll the windows up. Awad lit the joint and took a few hits and passed it to me. Asad changed lanes and the Taurus passed under the Hollywood Freeway interchange sign. I passed the joint to Asad, who inhaled a few puffs from the joint. I began to feel light-headed but relaxed. Images of Hada began to enter my mind again. I looked at my watch. It was 5:30 a.m.

Awad poured some more lines of coke onto the CD cover. He made four small lines and then bent his head forward. He lifted the CD cover close to his right nostril and snorted a line of caviar cocaine through a one dollar bill up into his nostril. Then he sniffed another line of cocaine and held the CD cover, with two remaining lines of cocaine toward Asad. I started laughing again. The green apple taste of Hada's lips had never tasted better. Asad, while driving and looking straight ahead, slightly leaned forward and sniffed the two remaining lines of cocaine on the CD cover held toward his face by Awad. After the balancing act had been completed, I noticed a small grin on Asad's face. The cocaine had taken its effect and I had forgotten all about Hada's kiss and how my nightmares began.

CHAPTER 8

HOW NIGHTS MANY HAD I SPENT LIKE THAT? I couldn't remember. The party again or maybe this one was more recent. Jober and I had paid a surprise visit to Johanna to see if she had any weed to smoke. We knocked on her door. Johanna answered with her usual glee and more so because she hadn't seen Jober for a while. A conversation was sparked that wouldn't end for the rest of the night. Johanna wanted to get high and so they all did, passing around the pipe again. Johanna always had good weed and this was good stuff especially since Nate Bob was gone back to Iowa so she had to get the weed while it was here in California.

"You guys want to go to a party?" Johanna asked Jober and me.

"Where is it?" asked Jober, who was very particular about where he went and with whom.

"It's off of Western. It's a house party and a Colombian group called Very Be Careful is going to be playing."

"I think I heard of them before," said Jober thinking.

They got themselves ready and left. It was another Friday night. It didn't take them long to get to Western, the hard part was going to be trying to find parking. We lucked out and found a spot two blocks away from the party. We hurried toward their destination, crossing Western carefully. The party was located on the second floor of an apartment building and it looked like a store was below. We went up the stairs. I noticed that one of the steps had been hollowed out with a glass front and a skull inside. It looked very psychedelic and the party was crowded and the party was actually two apartments with the front doors open. There was a band playing in one room and a bar was in both. I and Jober immediately bought beers and started talking about life. Johanna took off. Jober and I decided to follow her to the other side. The party looked more like a living room. There were some cages in the corner and I went to inspect them. There was nothing inside the cages that he could see except for some twigs, maybe a lizard lived in one of them at one time. Jober could smell weed and saw someone in the corner with a pipe. The music was getting louder and louder. This was just one of those parties that only certain people knew about. It felt good to be out and around people. The scene didn't seem typical of Los Angeles and everyone looked like they were someplace else and they probably were. Jober and I needed more drinks. I bought a Scotch and coke and Jober ordered a Midori Sour. We were both craving weed. I approached the guy with the pipe and asked him if I could smoke a little weed. He agreed and smoked me out. Jober arrived and we all started smoking and talking. It turns out that the guy knew Jober. Small world, I thought. The party was heating up.

Jober loved to watch *Goodfellas* and had recorded a good portion of the movie on his music sampler. "Son of gangster," he would sometimes say around his apartment.

He would often describe the family barbeques he would have at this house in Colombia and the swimming pool filled with guests. The hot tropical son beaming and crates of beer beyond drinkability.

"What did your parents do?"

"My dad was a narco trafficker," Jober said to me.

I was drinking Scotch and Coke. It had become my favorite drink. For some reason it took what seemed like minutes for the information to compute inside of my brain.

"Yeah," I said.

"Yeah!" said Jober.

Jober needed to find a bathroom and waited in line before entering it. He came back to me and told me to check out the bathroom because it had these cool Polaroids. I went to investigate and found a series of Polaroid shots of blood in a sink and some cocaine Jober left. I took it and snorted it. It was now time to go to the other side. The band was about to start. Jober found me and we made our way through the crowd and to the other apartment.

"You've known me all this time and you didn't tell me," I said, drifting.

"I didn't know what to say. I thought you would put all the pieces together," said Jober looking at the party.

There was something about our apartment building that allowed it to yield so many delights. The cache of books that I had found in the basement of my apartment building was the other one. Sometime after moving into the building I had decided to explore it. It was a new situation for me. I hadn't quite started to teach yet but I had found a room in the basement and it was full of books, all of the classics, from Homer to Richard Wright. It couldn't have come at a better time. This tomb of knowledge that I had found was like finding the Ark of the Covenant. Whoever the man was that had left these books was of the same making as me, yet greater. He was obviously African-American and he was well read of German, French and even Russian. There were book titles in each language scattered about. I grabbed what I could and retreated to my room.

Finding those books was like finding Jober, who was straight out of the jungles of South America and suburban California. It was such an odd treasure. The books I had found revealed as much about life as Jober's attitudes and beliefs revealed about him. That all the limitations that he had found of life had not impeded on others. That there were places that he had to go and see and hadn't. It worked on his mind. I looked at Jober very differently now. This time it was just that all of the stories made sense now the cars and the guests and the strange things that happened at his family's house in Cali, Colombia.

"My mother has told me more about it since I had been here," said Jober casually drinking his Midori Sour. I hadn't expected this that night. But for some reason it looked like things were starting to crumble away. That I knew that Jober would return to Cali and I had told him that he was would. America was too restrictive. There was a different kind of social cohesion that existed in Cali.

The party was packed but dark. It hadn't reached its climax. Things couldn't have gotten any more exciting than they are now except for a few little Christmas lights. After a while everything just became a whirl. The party climaxed and the flow of energy gripped me and I didn't want to let go of. It's when one forgot about time. That's the best type of feeling to have. When time didn't matter. When you didn't need a watch. When the spontaneity kept you wide awake and in your dreams. When things happened that you didn't expect. Making friends and losing your money or your keys as if they had somehow walked away. That you can have friends and feel alone and even in a group of people, the city bearing down on you. That those who could accomplish this balancing act somehow made themselves appear more superior. That there was a point at which one could not cry as much as one wanted to. Colombia awaited me playing on my mind and danced like a nude woman in the pupils of Jober's eyes.

I was trying not to let certain things matter to me anymore. That if I could somehow live a clear life free from all of my anxieties and preoccupations I could be free. Alcohol and marijuana were in everyone's eyes. The music ticked exact like a clock. The slight click of the percussion instruments, which had been brought to Latin America by African slaves long ago and the bass made you want to move your hips. There was no way to fight the groove of the music. It was simple but kind to the spirit, like water. The crowd responded with coolness and gyrating hips. This type of Colombian folk music was familiar to Jober but he once had rejected it, now he savored it. He was now more appreciative of it. There were parts of life that I knew nothing about just as I yearned to travel. The two of us learned from each other a thing or two about life. It was a book you couldn't put down and a plane ticket you had to take. Nobody wanted to be uncool and everyone wanted to be liked while disguising their ignorance.

Jober began dancing with Johanna and I saw a black girl and asked her to dance with me. She agreed. Dancing with her was like riding a wave. One had to be on time and then it was fun and you could find yourself moving in all directions. I asked her for her phone number. She took out her cell phone and punched into my phone number and she said she would call me and vanished. I liked her short Afro. She was definitely different and I was definitely drunk. There was something she was trying to tell me but I couldn't hear her. The room was filled with weed and cigarette smoke and people. She kissed my cheek and walked out of the party.

I hadn't expected anything like this to happen but it had arrived just in time to calm my nerves. Just when it seemed like life was taking a downturn, something might arrive to pick things up a bit. It was a surprise party. If only life could be like this all the time. People dancing and frosting on the cake, everyone smiling and getting along. Lots of people around like a birthday party. Was there any escape from getting older and realizing that time was passing you and would lap you?

CHAPTER 9

Jober flipped channels on the television. Another situation had arisen. Jober had moved back to the city after he had moved back to Montrose. That had occurred in the summer but not before Gino had come from Cali.

Gino was twenty-three years old and the only guy that could beat Jober at video games. He was also a bass player for a popular Colombian punk rock band Las Rudas. One day I had met Gino on the roof. I had rolled two blunts and when I got on the roof there was Gino wearing a black motorcycle jacket with sideburns and mid-length hair. His Wayfarer glasses were pitch black and blocking his eyes. He had arrived in the middle of the night from Texas now he was on the top of the roof of an apartment building and about to get very high on some weed from Rambo.

Gino who had had many adventures with Jober in Cali and they had even played music together. I had seen pictures of him before on the slides that Jober had developed and put into his Macintosh computer. All the pictures seemed to be coming closer together. There were still people Jober hadn't seen but maybe one day he would know.

The three of us smoke pot and looked out on the view

from the roof. Gino who was crazy and didn't look it one bit but loved comic books, blondes and rock n roll. Gino who tried to give an old color TV to a prostitute in front of our building in exchange for a blowjob. Jober was interpreting this as he did at home but Gino arriving somehow didn't jive with him but Gino was here in the states and was trying to get a job and get some money to send back home. His girlfriend and daughter had moved in with him in Cali but were now living with his brother in Cali. Gino talked about his daughter all the time but he didn't like his ex-girlfriend's lifestyle and like most people they had split up. Gino was responsible. He brought money with him but he needed a lot more to make this trip and his brother had been to the states in New York before but got deported, so he felt he would do things differently this time. The smoke blew from their noses and lips.

Soon Gino was hanging out with Johanna and Paul who had just moved in downstairs, a dread from Baltimore. They started all gathering on the roof. I had a lot of time on my hands. I had just paid for his emergency teaching credential and had had a lot of days off from work. We drank Colombian, Domecq brandy every night and beer and smoked pot and brought a radio on the roof and started listening to music and partying into the night. We smoked more weed than we could consume. There seemed no end to the conversations, beer and weed.

Jober went to bed early and was very regimented. Gino and I would walk through the night until they would reach Tommy Burgers and we might share a chili cheeseburgers with fries and a Hawaiian punch and then return to his apartment and drink Domecq brandy and talk about comic books.

"Has Jober ever smoked crack?" Gino asked me. It seemed like a weird question.

"No, not that I know of," I said, but Jober had expressed the desire to try it, something which Gino thought was fucking crazy. It seemed like Jober wanted to try everything. Jober existed in a world where there were no limits. Gino was very similar but different, than Jober which probably led to their arguments and which eventually led to Gino going back home to Cali after he had gotten a shitty construction job with the help of Jober mother's boyfriend, who one time pushed Jober into the couch for being a smartass. Jober was arrogant and liked to swing his intellect around and speak pompously about all the things he had seen from traveling because he had the means to do it or live it. Gino couldn't be more aware of the living situation with Jober was starting to boil over. Gino's job was a long commute. He seemed to take everything in stride. I knew he was worried about his daughter. Everything was new. I could see him landing in Texas straight out of Colombia and everyone around him wearing cowboy hats but he made it. We smoked out daily and drank Domecq brandy. He had brought several bottles from Cali. The stuff tasted like sweet cough syrup. Gino could drink it like Kool-Aid. I wasn't as talented. One night we all found ourselves on the roof and we were partying and drinking. It was a cool night. Everyone was there, mostly people that don't even live here anymore, but they were the cool people in the building. We had several blunts and E & J Brandy and more Domecq. Everybody was talking with Gino because he had just arrived and it seemed like perfect timing and the perfect place. You get off of a plane and you're immediately in a place where people smoke a lot of weed and make a lot of music. Artist and everyone could probably here us and the music echoing in the night. We didn't care and it didn't matter. Josh had decided that we should go out. He knew of a club that was free to get in. It was across town and some of us decided to go. It was already 2 a.m. We got our stuff and left and met downstairs in the lobby. Josh was parked in the back of the motel next door. The owner of the motel let people park back there but they had to pay a monthly fee. It was hard to find parking around the building and especially at night when you were in a hurry and wanted to get out of the street and into the building. We walked next door and headed for Josh's car and passed a group of guys who were hanging out. Something about them didn't seem right and it wasn't because as soon as we got in Josh's Explorer I heard, "Bad news, esse!" They had us surrounded and asked for our money. One guy even came as far into the car to search us. I didn't have any money on me but I had my passport in my back pocket because I had lost my driver's license. It was crazy. We got out of the SUV and at one point I thought we might try and fight back in retaliation but then one of the cholos flashed his gun and then the bandits took off. Josh went after one of them and swung at them but we called him back to his car and he came back and got in it. We were all in shock. I was speechless. I didn't know what to say but I thought of only one thing and that was revenge and I wished for a moment to have a gun at that instance so that I could kill them. The bandits ran off and a taxicab blocked us in. The wild west had not faded one bit and we had been ambushed like settlers on the Oregon Trail. We were all devastated and we decided that we should go home and call the police who arrived later and question all everyone except me and Gino. I was a little frustrated at how the police reacted to me, a frustration about not being heard. Ignored. I had felt this way before, like talking too much in the classroom and students tuning me out, ignoring me. I know for Gino this whole experience was extraordinary because he had come all the way from Cali, Colombia only to be robbed in America.

That night we had all become brothers and solidified our relationship. I thought this is what Gino was trying to escape from and that he came from one of the most dangerous places in the world but America should also be on that list. Gino and I gave the police our addresses and then went to his apartment. Jober was asleep. We woke him up and he seemed a little pissed off. Gino told him in Spanish and in English what had happened. All we wanted to do was get high. We went to Paul's apartment and started drinking and smoking more pot. We were all too tired we all went home and promised to get together the next day. It was daylight. I couldn't sleep. I felt like I was going mad. My life had always been important to me but that importance took on a new meaning. I realized how vulnerable we are all but somehow we exist in the world of careful cohesion and social engineering. The allusion was greater than the reality of our lives. That death stalked us all every day was there. I lay in bed that morning thinking about being dead and I had gotten shot or if I had saved us all or took the gun away from the guy and put it up his asshole and pulled the trigger like in the movie *Baise Moi*. The next night we had gathered on the roof. Mike brought out his best hip-hop and old school disc that he could make and we had Bartles & Jaymes and blunts and more Domecq and we started drinking and talking about revenge.

"Man, if I had my gun that whole situation would have been different!" said Mike who now distrusted every guy he saw with a shaved head.

"Those guys were fucked up man," said Gino in his Cali accent.

The truth was that we were all pissed and felt violated. What could we do now?

"Fuck the Star Motel," said Josh, who then took a beer bottle and hurled it at the roof of the Burger King, where it shattered into a million little pieces. Gino threw his down on the roof of the motel and then we all laughed and had rounds of brandy. Susan couldn't believe that all of us guys got robbed and didn't do anything. She came over and sat on my couch in my apartment and put her head on my chest. A green strand of her highlighted hair stuck to my face. She moved it away and closed her green eyes. If she only knew how frustrated we were of the same fact. Los Angeles had revealed its coldness once again and we had all felt its sting. It was something that one doesn't take lightly. Living each day in Los Angeles was hard enough and then to have to contend with bandits and other scumbags out to profit on your misfortune, making things even more complicated.

Gino had seen worse, like walking home and having a gangster point a nine-millimeter Beretta at you from the driver's side window of his SUV and pull the trigger. There were no bullets in the gun and then the guy drives off laughing like, treating you like a used condom. Life seemed cheap in Cali but then life was cheap in Los Angeles too at times and not every murder made the headlines and it just seemed like it wasn't supposed to happen here in America. Bullshit!

We continued to drink our pain away and became tighter and everything else seemed just irrelevant especially after almost losing your life, you started to wonder if all the other bullshit that you worried about each day wasn't just a waste of time. These thought just kept crossing my mind. Jober just seemed not to have any comment at all. What could he say? He wasn't there and he seemed so distant at this time, though when he was off work we would all somehow manage to hang out, maybe go to an arcade across from Los Angeles Community college and play Sniper video games or other games trying to get high scores. We would go score from Rambo and then go smoke out and go to the guitar center. One time we went and this tall blonde girl pulls up in a Mercedes SUV walks into the place and starts drumming out of control and we had both entered the Guitar Center at the same time and go our separate ways but end up in the drum section and then we're all drumming away and playing different beats and it's kind of strange and people are digging it. All that shit didn't matter now. We were alive and we're going to try a little bit harder not to take it all for granted.

I spent a night away from the group and I met up with Asad in Santa Monica. He was now driving a taxi. We decided to go to Habibi, a shee sha house where they had hookas and you could smoke flavored tobacco and drink teas and have other types of Arabic food. It was popular place and it was always packed and open-air constructed. The Arabic music was blasting. You could play backgammon and chess and there were mirrors and everyone was looking cool and checking everybody out and trying not to be so obvious about it. There were Americans there too. It was next to UCLA in the village where the students went to shop and let off steam. There were a lot of other Middle Eastern cultures there too and the women went out of their way to look like pieces of candy. After seeing so many voluptuous bodies your eyes would continuously wander as you gazed at all the ladies with round full figures, looking like ice cream and cake. There were four of us, Ali, Awad, Mohammad and me. I had told Asad about being robbed and he felt sorry for me. We had smoked pot earlier before arriving there and found a table inside. I was still in a little bit of a state of shock but Asad thought of his way to make things interesting by playing congas provided by the café that was owned by an Egyptian, with a long gray ponytail. A girl then stood up and started dancing and gyrating her hips like a belly dancer and got more into it and then the girl stood on a table. She wore low-cut midriffs corduroy pants and her red underwear peaked out over the top of her jeans as she continued to gyrate her hips to the beat of the music coming from the stereo and Asad beating on the congas. He stood up and started to dance with her and people started clapping and you could feel all of this energy between their bodies. Then he sat down and another girl stood up and she had wider hips and she started gravitating toward them and it seemed we were all fixed on her hips and I felt an erection and the tobacco swirling in my head. Others just stared at the scene with smiles on their faces. Then Asad stopped drumming and the girl stopped dancing and asked why he had stopped tapping and it was because the song had changed, creating a different beat and throwing him off tempo. The girl sat down and started talking to her friends who just smiled and acted aloof. Asad struck up a conversation with her and she seemed friendly. She was Persian as were her friends. Another girl was sitting next to me and she was quiet and Mohammad had stepped on my foot underneath the table and at first I was angered by this but he was just amazed at how much had been happening in the next few days. Mohammad had found that the girl was from Iraq and sometimes frequented Habibi but she seemed rather coy and a little put off by the confidence of Mohammad who was married already but it didn't seemed to matter now because his wife was at home and she was Vietnamese.

Samira was the name of the Iraqi girl. She seemed so quiet and got up out of her seat and rubbed her hips on my left shoulder as she left to go to the bathroom and then when she returned to her seat had done it again and then turned and continued to talk to Mohammad. She bent down to adjust her hooka and flashed her large breasts held firm in a tight bra towards my eyes; I seemed almost paralyzed and unresponsive at such delights as Asad started flirting with the dancer with his drum beats and her friends, one of which had dyed-blonde hair and was wearing low-cut jeans, her silver G-string poking above the sides of her jeans. She let off little glances and turned to smile at her friends but when Samira had sat down she made sure to cut her off from our view. At first Mohammad thought that she was with a guy who was sitting across from her but he seemed to be only a friend. They chatted some more as Mohammad talked with Asad and drank tea and thought about the last two days and what had just happened. The music continued sometimes repeating but it didn't matter to the smoke-filled minds of the patrons who smoked different flavored she-sha and gossiped. New patrons came and went as the hours passed. It wasn't cheap but then this might be the closest you get to the Middle East. It had turned out to be a cool night. I was not missing a beat on the beauty before me, like some story from *1001 Nights* had become reality.

It was time to leave.

I missed Susan.

Nothing had changed back at home. Jober had gone to a barbeque at his grandmother's and then to meet with his sisters afterward who babysat for the regional president of Wells Fargo. He had a house with a pool and well Jober had mentioned it before but it seemed that it would be one afternoon without me, who suspected that meeting with his grandmother would just not be possible. That would have just been too controversial. Jober's mother's descendants had been slave owners and Jober had a copy of an old will written some time during slavery that mentioned the name of slaves and who they would be given to after their master had died. It was strange for me to see such a document and then think to the present, the descendants of two very different but similar American families now dealing with life had come up before in I and Jober's conversation. At times it seemed that Jober was so ignorant about basic facts of life and in others he was so well educated.

"A slave was still not free," I said in response to Jober's excuse for slavery, after he said that slaves were provided for, as if that somehow lessoned the brutality of slavery.

It all really made me wonder what type of life had Jober really been living but it must have been one prior to the meeting of someone sheltered from African-American culture. And well Jober said it would be good for me to go to Colombia because blacks in Cali, were not empowered and it would be good for them to see me. Another strange revelation by Jober who was as eccentric as I was also subconscious about my own cultural identity. Some things I took as genuine curiosity or the desire to understand something about African-American culture such as his desire to hear rap, something he knew little or nothing about and was just as inept about race relations. This was an opportunity for him to learn something and for me to learn something about how important social class is entrenched in American society and beyond. Something that most people don't really talk about but is the reality of life not only in America but all of the world and that we were no longer the good guys but over fed, spoiled kids.

CHAPTER 10

The building was changing and Jober told me that he thought that he wanted to move and started looking for apartments. Gino and Jober were barely tolerating each other but they were also the greatest of friends. The story about being stuck up by a knife-wielding robber and Gino taking the knife away from him and then he started fighting the thief with his belt. There were more revelations. I couldn't remember them all and the robbery faded like other memories and even further while I visited New Orleans with my mother. Susan had gone back to Baltimore. She wrote me letters and revealed to me that she had lupus and had lost her hair and had been undergoing treatments. Her cousin wrote for the *Times Picayune*. She said I should contact him. I wrote back to her. She said don't give up and when she was well maybe I could visit her in Baltimore. I made a video of her roller-skating in Eagle Rock, at a roller rink. I kept watching it over and over, looking at the smile on her face.

Things were slowing down and most of that had to do with the terrorist attack on September 11. Paul had called me and told me to get up and come over. I didn't have cable. I put on a shirt that had the initials N and Y in capitals letters side by side. The T-shirt was white. I looked at one of Susan's letters one last time, glanced at Iko's picture on the refrigerator and then I left my apartment and went downstairs and looked at the television at Paul's.

"Look at this shit man," said Paul.

I looked at the large screened television that Paul used to play endless video games on. Dominating the screen was an image of one of the World Trade center buildings being rammed by an airliner. It was an apocalyptic event. People were running everywhere on the screen, the air was gray and people were covered in dust and debris. Then another airliner crashed into the other tower and exploded and the top of the building came crashing down on people below. People jumped out of the windows of the other buildings. Everyone was speechless. Paul was drinking brandy and had given everyone a glass. It was a horrible sight, terrifying. Information was flashed and moved across the bottom of the screen as a newscaster tried to put into words the unspeakable. I couldn't comment. This was an act of war, I thought. It was World War Three but not how I thought it was going to happen. It was being propagandized as an act of terrorism. Another plane crashed into the pentagon and another plane crashed in Pennsylvania and speculation that the airplane was headed for the White House, but it crashed and a cell phone call from one of the passengers spoke of an attempt to subdue a high-jacker before the plane crashed. The conversation wasn't heard but filtered by the correspondent. It was crazy. The unimaginable had happened. I had thought that since the last presidential election and all the controversy surrounding it that after that day things would never be the same and indeed they were not. And people were for the first time confronted with political corruption for the whole world to see. Though they had recounted and recounted ballots it was obvious that the American people had been swindled somehow and really do about it knew how much the rest of the world really thought about us.

Bang!

Lisa Gonzales was twenty-three, Puerto-Rican and Mexican, beautiful, and conscientious. Her hair was black and somewhat brown and her eyes were wide and brown and shined like stars. Her body was like an hourglass. I liked her and had confessed my emotions to Lisa on a bus back from the Mexican Border. It had been a long day of protests against the INS for their treatment of border crossers and the whole immigration system. It was a two-hour bus ride from Los Angeles to San Yisidro filled with trade unionists, students, socialists, educators, communists, and others. They sang songs and ate food to soften their anticipation of meeting other leftist groups and organizations that had gathered at the border. Some would go farther and cross the border. The police had shown up and had massed a large battalion of men in riot gear. Some were headed for the border area where protesters went and others had stayed at the park where I and Lisa had finally arrived. There was a stage and a band and a PA system and lots of people and video cameras and people gathering information and receiving it in various ways. It was a beautiful day. Lisa was happy and aloof. She talked in Spanish on her cell phone during part of the journey to the border. I had turned on camcorder and captured her eloquent Spanish. Lisa was so mischievous and cunning and had a natural talent for organizing people. She kept a stable of men hanging on her every word. She was as voluptuous as she was intelligent. Her frankness was acute and her girlish outbursts made her attractive. She had discovered me at a school while I was subbing and she liked how I bonded with the students. We saw each other in the teachers' cafeteria, instantly communicating with one another. She said she was a dancer and I said I was writer. Lisa had organized a poetry circle at Olvera Street at La Boca Café. It also doubled as a gallery. It was a spiritual place. There was coffee and expressos and Mexican antique and contemporary art everywhere. You never knew who was going to show up. Like the Castaneda disciple who arrived like a brujo out of the cold October night. It was raining but there he was. Talking about Aztec magic and cleaning and cleansing oneself of the pasts, strange physical and metaphysical exercises and harnessing energy. I drank my coffee and watched the magician as he watched Lisa. Lisa and I were the only two left. Lisa had agreed to lock the café up and its owner Don Yanez had gone home. Then the wizard was gone, just as soon as it seemed he had arrived to maybe to bring havoc. But he brought wisdom and understanding and something new to the table. I copied down when the next gathering of Castaneda disciples would gather, the closest location being in Mexico City, another was in Amsterdam. Lisa looked at me who thought that only such a thing could happen with her because she had some type of cosmic energy that no other girl carried along with her.

There was some power in her. It could have been her eyes or hippie-like ways. Her unshaved armpits and round Puerto-Rican-Mexican breasts that looked like half cantaloupes. She had the best and the worst of the Spaniards, their rudeness, but the hardness of an Indian and the beauty of the combination.

I felt inspired to write more poetry now and had made new friends, who liked my poetry and candid rhetorical style. There were Spaniards there too, who made Spain even closer to me. Iona was one, a singer and a little plump. Lisa later expelled her from the group because she felt that she was just trying to promote her singing. Iona did and was and called me to talk about it. She liked me and had invited him to her birthday party. I brought Nora and Iona, sang corridos in her party dress at 1 a.m. Her Spanish friends had gathered around and there was drinking and cake and food and Madonna music and people were having a great time and I got high with the Nora a Korean girl from work who on our way to the beach talked about hanging out in Beverly Hills with Israelis, coke parties and drug dealers. She drove my Spanish friends to indifference. It was a mixed night. The frosting Iona's friend put on my face and Nora's face couldn't have been stranger. The awkward feeling it gave me. It was suggestive and erotic. I had asked her in Spanish if she wanted to get high with us and she just smiled as if she didn't hear me and I took pictures. My friend had driven us to the party. He liked Nora but I wouldn't let him have her. He was a great guitar player. I wanted Nora for myself. The Spaniards knew how to party and had invited me and my friend to the Spanish Club at USC, organized by the Spanish Consulate and the Counsel General had come on one occasion. People didn't speak in English and I let my camera run and I also talked. I remembered when I had shown up that day and Iona had finally arrived and she wore a nice red dress and had only black eyeliner around her eyes that somewhat extended from beyond the reaches of her eyes. The dress accentuated the curves in her body and one might think of the power of Clydesdale horse. Iona could sing and could act and was also an English teacher at a middle school in Compton as part of an exchange program. Her first play was a Shakespeare play, *The Taming of The Shrew*. There was an after party for the actors and actresses. They talked and I was high. Now Iona was gone and Lisa and I had fought one night but before that things were cool. Lisa had invited me to a sweat lodge. I picked her up at her house. She was always fighting with her mother but in reality Lisa was as critical as her mother. Lisa had been accepted to Berkeley and it was now a matter of time before we would be apart and our meeting at the library was really our goodbye.

At the sweat lodge in Oxnard, my car had given him trouble and he remembered coming to her house. The nice tree-lined streets and her immaculate house. Meeting her brother and her father who were so friendly. Her mother's dark shades that she wore around the house. Lisa wore a large serape and looked like a revolutionary and she was and well read and articulate in English, Spanish, and French. She criticized me constantly to the limits of torture but I was gracious even after she told me in my kitchen apartment that she didn't want sex. That was okay with me now and I could wait for her but not too long. I fantasized about being Dustin Hoffman in *The Graduate* and rushing to Berkeley in a fiat roadster to meet her and to stop her from marrying some bourgeois pig. That would be so fucking groovy. I could see it now. I liked to think of her that way. She read part of my novel and said it was degrading to women but I took it as a compliment because I had achieved the desired effect. She was too close to my heart when she came over one night and then she wanted cigarettes and then we went for a walk to a gas station and she started talking to people on the street longer than usual and about this and that in Spanish and some part of her abstract nature made her tantalizing and ubiquitous, like hearing her say "mommi" to her mother on the phone. She walked fast away from me and I pursued her, and she went faster just short of running teasing me to catch up. Some man was driving by and observed us on the street and slowed down a couple of times to offer her a ride. I became furious just short of slapping her in the face. But then we finally made it back to my apartment but not before she sat down at a bus stop and was approached by a vagrant who asked her for a cigarette which she lit for him and she smoked there patiently at the bus stop and all I could think of was getting home. If only I had the nerve to slap her or fuck her through her nice ass in retribution.

I told her about that night sometime after it had passed and she tried to amuse herself during our conversation about the experience but I told her that if she ever did it again I would slap the shit out of her. She was shocked and told me not to talk to her that way and then I left her car and she drove away in her Volvo. She came back the next day and talked to me. I met her in the parking lot next to my apartment. She brought some red beans and rice and was dressed like a little girl with black leggings and wearing a denim one-piece miniskirt I wanted to lift her skirt up in the Burger King parking lot and fuck her. She wouldn't let me touch her. We went to a café. Before we went home, we sat in her Volvo silently. She pulled her skirt back a little bit so I could see her panties and then she moved the edge of her skirt back. I leaned forward to kiss her but she slowly put her hand on my mouth and pushed me back in my seat. It was raining a little bit outside. We sat there for a while and then she drove me home listening to Spanish music.

I missed Lisa. There were no more Café La Boca's. No more poetry nights. No more crazy Spaniards. It was just me and my memories of the city and what her face looked like. The last time we spoke she had called my sister first because she didn't have my new number and they spoke on the phone but she didn't want to see me because she said she was fat. She got kicked out of her UC Berkeley dormitory for having candles burning in her room. She was eccentric like me but she always had to be the leader, was intellectually domineering and was deeply entrenched in her indigenous spirituality and kept alters for Día de Los Muertos.

CHAPTER 11

There was a homeless man who would often sit out front on a planter in front of our building. A lot of people used that spot for depot. I had walked past it several times without making it so important. That was until I had met John. I didn't know till later that there might have been something wrong with him but like in all relationships you never really see anything until later. But up to that point it was just another adventure in the building. This was before Jober and before Paul. It was in the early stages. I was jumping around a little bit but that's because of all these dreams and sometimes nightmares that I was having.

Where did the stories end or begin? Sometimes you don't want to know. You just want to see what you want to believe. John drove a black Volvo. I used to smoke weed in front of the building on the stoop. It's how I met so many friends and acquaintances. I was just about to finish a joint when he had arrived. He looked like a cartoon character or like a young Ted Kennedy. His family was upper-middle class and when I saw his parents one day, they were silent and looked worried about him.

"Shannon Doherty's bodyguards beat me up," he said.

"Really? Why?" I asked.

"They were just being assholes," he responded.

It didn't seem to make sense. He said they beat him up in front of a club. I was wondering if he was going to sue or something. I think I asked him that but the reply was always somehow stating that it was going to happen. We started rolling blunts. I taught but I also had days when I had so much time on my hands that I could do whatever I wanted. I smoked pot almost every day. It was my entertainment but it was also a type of adventure because of all the characters that I knew from smoking weed but at the moment it was living in this building that had created so many scenarios. John was a part of this whole story but only temporarily. We smoked out a lot and then we went on missions around the city smoking and driving and talking about things. It was like being a kid again and at that moment I had forgotten about Iko. The small bird that I had held so tightly in my hand was now free. I didn't know what I was doing but it was better than setting myself on fire like a protesting monk during the Vietnam War.

John had many interesting friends and enemies. There were dozens of transients and other characters by our building and even more so because of the low-budget motel that was next door where I was eventually mugged with my friends. I started to see some of these people in the building and they were with John. His apartment was filled with things that I felt should not have been there. It seemed like more of a museum than anything else. What struck me most was the California flag that hung in the corner of his apartment. The place was squalid. We sat on chairs from a 1970's dining room set with linoleum-like padding, fastened to the sides with screws. I remembered that we had similar chairs at home when I was young and I always had to press the middle padding back into place and refasten the screws.

There in the living room was a man I had filmed with my new video camera from the roof fighting with some prostitute. Now he was here in front of me unaware of what I knew about him but I was smoking a blunt with this guy and talking to him. John knew everyone and let everyone into his apartment to smoke crack or weed or take a shower. And so the cement planter was some sort of beacon where I had passed people before and now I would see them in John's apartment and I suspected that John smoked crack himself. Something wasn't right but my curiosity led me deeper into trying to take it all in.

CHAPTER 12

Juan Pablo was someone that I had known for a long time. We had grown up in the same neighborhood and graduated from the same high school. We were both from the city and shared its mentality. Juan was originally from New York and had moved to Los Angeles a few years earlier than me. Somehow they had found each other at school and in the same neighborhood where I did, not too far away from today.

Juan Pablo always talked about sex and he was in real estate now but had committed fraud and so now he was practicing real estate illegally. When he fucked women he liked to do it in places that were so obvious that you probably wouldn't notice. Now he's dating a girl and they met at a club and she was wearing a dress that night and a fight started outside the club and the police came and a crowd gathered and she was giving him blowjob on the side of his car.

That's Juan Pablo.

I think he fucked his way through high school. The first time I had sex was in college but I can't even count the number of girls he fucked at our school. Now he has a son, he's a regular guy, drives a jag, we eat lunch and talk shit.

He's like a brother to me. He tells me not to worry about my loneliness and that it's all inside of my head and that he envies me. Now, I could never figure out why he would envy me. Everything in my life has happened so late. I don't get it at all. When I'm a hundred years old I'll have a harem. I don't understand it and when I meet women they always live so fucking far away and I don't drive and so the torture just builds and builds. My conservatism works against me but Pablo says that I'm too conservative. A two headed beast that I see every day when I wake up in the morning. It looks me in the face and smiles at me. I can see it through the window superimposed over the city. My skin is burning at night because it's so cold. I can feel myself cracking away. Pablo takes it all in stride. Everything we learned about women wasn't true—they are like men and they don't give a fuck and they want it right now. It's just that men are so brainwashed. Pablo could talk for hours. Girls giving him the blues but it's always been that way with him. Before we would walk for a long time and drink and now we're driving or we're doing things in style and eating at some Cuban joint and loving the food and staring at women's asses and comparing them and our dicks are so hard we could crack tiles. These women all the time looking like ice cream and cake and loving it and men crash their cars and go to war over a bitch. I was speechless. I was actually enjoying my solitude and I was starting to awaken myself. I felt like I had been in hibernation or something. The whole world frozen over that's how I felt in the hospital waiting to be tested for a STD or being completely thawed after screwing Monique. I could feel her breaking in half after putting her legs in the air like Iko had done but she didn't bleed and then she went limp and passed out. She laid there for a while with her eyes closed, unmoving. Only a few minutes before she had been moaning in a low voice and then she looked dead.

"Holy shit!" says Juan Pablo. "You fucked her too hard!"

"I ran into my old girlfriend," I said smiling. "She's still talking about the past and how she has a new man now but he doesn't know my dick was in her mouth. What a crazy bitch!"

I could only smile or laugh when Juan Pablo talked about such escapades. There was a life here that I wasn't living and Juan Pablo was, but that didn't stop us from having the almost familiar relationship. There was something in Juan Pablo that was almost like a brother to me because it was Juan Pablo that had pulled me out of my shell so long ago when I had arrived so sullenly to Los Angeles as alien, as Juan Pablo had been when he had travelled across the country to Los Angeles in a van with his mother and younger brother. His eldest sister had stayed in New York.

"Fuck that! Ciao!" They were gone and once again life continues.

Juan Pablo had tried everything, even trying to get me to fuck the girlfriend of a local cholo from MS, a local gang in our barrio. She came over with her friend wearing high heels and a miniskirt but just before conversation turned serious, my mother had come home and being the kind woman and mother that she is, offered them all drinks.

"Your mother is cool" is all any of them could say. They took off feeling a little uncomfortable. She later called me.

"Are you sure you're a virgin? I can't believe it!" she said partially in Spanish and English. "Don't worry about it, it won't be that bad. We can fuck!" She hung up the phone and I came on myself.

That was the end of the conversation. That was a good thing because who she was didn't seem to faze Juan Pablo. I was terrified but excited at the possibility of screwing the girlfriend of a notorious gangster from our neighborhood. Juan Pablo had saved a girl from being raped at a ditching party. The girl thanked him but he said he screwed her through her asshole and she gave him a blowjob and then he gave her bus fair and sent her home alone. I had never heard anything like that nor was I living that kind of life in my previous high school until I met Juan Pablo in Southern California. I spent most of my time at home reading comic books or Mishima novels from the school library or cutting class. My mother was worried but I had good grades so she left me alone. I hated high school in the Bay Area and it hated me back but I was having fun for the first time in my life, living in Los Angeles. I had moments of glory but mostly I had longings to be someplace else the same way that Jober felt longing to be away, back in Cali, Colombia. To be back in the tropical heat where his friends and I drove through the city at night smoking a huge joint maybe rolled by some Colombian woman or teenage girl who could take the skin off of a Pial Roja cigarette and roll a perfect joint with Colombian marijuana and who made J-Lo look like Shakira on crack. There was no comparison.

See, Juan Pablo is the kind guy who has fucked girls in shopping malls while security guards were walking around. He would just tell the girl to wear a dress and a G-string and to sit on his lap and then he'd fuck her while kids were walking by eating ice cream or riding skateboards. I had only fucked a girl in a movie theater but that was pushing it.

French Extract

The next day Jober told me that Naomi was in Paris but coming to Los Angeles. It had been a long time for her but she welcomed the opportunity to try and keep her relationship with Jober intact. Life had taught her and the rest of us that long-distance relationships don't work. For some they work but for most of us it just didn't work. Naomi was in Los Angeles and was expected and unexpected. She was Jober's ex-girlfriend. I remember when she finally arrived. She surprised him at his house. Jasmin would arrive a few days later. It was really a reunion of old friends and lovers and the passion they shared for their relationships was uninhibited by distance. I saw it all from a distance but friendship was real and you knew it when you tasted it. You didn't have to look for it. There was a lot of weed around and they were happy to meet me, such a contrast between me and Jober. Naomi watched my every movement, catching me off guard by mimicking me. Naomi was sexy and exotic and South American. Being amongst these friends was an experience that I was still learning to understand. Jober was younger than me but he was more livid and in the end this would spoil us like a wild mango as friends but at this time we were all free and seemed to be rolling down a grassy hill like little kids as was true of some of the pictures we had taken. Life had become cinematic for some of us. It was about how things looked not how things actually were in life. Reality was too harsh. Image and icon had become reality. There were different ways to live and every aspect of life had its limitations and this was the hardest part to realize. All relationships had limitations and when you reached the beach it was the same. The ocean was the most obvious and Naomi and Jober lost themselves in the gray sand far from the cities of the world and left the two writers alone. It couldn't have been more picturesque. At the beach dreams are made and reformed and all hope returns that isn't possible away from the power of the sea. There were other ways to live and that was something that life only offered occasionally. My life was becoming more international. There bubbled in me a longing to take off but responsibilities were painful and curiosity had no cure. The only answer lies in doing the impossible and only a few of us were likely to take the risk of exploring.

Jober had met up with Naomi in Paris and that meant something then. I listened to tales about Paris but was reminded that he would probably come to his own conclusion. It seemed magical. The second trip to Spain, old friends and old habits and new characters and the Spaniards' rudeness and humor confronted once again. The world seemed too large. I listened with envy. Jasmin made things more interesting. Another expatriate that had returned to North America. She was fluent in Spanish, voluptuous and as keenly intellectual as Jober was cunning. They made an awesome foursome and life melted away. Jasmin lived in New Jersey but was the daughter of American missionaries who had lived in Cali, Colombia at some time. She was Colombian but was as much an anomaly as Jober. I had become Rasputin in my own eyes. I felt like an outsider but that would only be natural. Jasmin leapt out at you like a Playboy centerfold. She had a zeitgeist, as they say, and you could see it in her eyes and her long blonde hair. She was too down to earth to have been created in any other way that seemed possible to me. There was the South American kinetic disposition that existed between them all. Jasmin headed south in the wintertime when the weather on the eastern coast of the United States became Antarctica. Her Spanish was spoken with a Colombian accent and was sensual and tropical and everything it made your feel when you heard it. I loved it and I couldn't get enough of the vibe I was feeling. It was great again knowing that you belonged that you had a place in life when otherwise you felt alienated and the limitations of passion confronted you with your own imagination. It was great to think about these times smoking pot with women and forget about time, the dream sheet thrown onto a bed. There was no time to think. I wondered if it was really happening. Jober's apartment smelled like chronic weed and when he lived in the same building as me it was not uncommon to find enough weed on the floor of his apartment to make a joint, which shocked Naomi. It was like a dream. Dealing with people from so far away makes it seem easier sometimes. Talking in person was so much more difficult. In the end I walked home alone through the cold night back to my apartment awaiting the next day. Wondering what happened. Walking was relaxing and I could savor all of my thoughts. There weren't too many people on the streets and maybe because the tendency to think that it was unsafe and was overbearing aunt; that's what made it so therapeutic to walk. Everything was temporary and soon Jasmin and Naomi would be gone. Colombia would dance before my eyes. This was the way to nirvana.

An eclipse was approaching too and I had discussed it with Jober and they were both going to try and view it. Finally it did arrive and was every bit miraculous and mysterious as it was propagandized to be. We had both been thinking about it and planning how each of them would see it. The events never seemed to stop presenting themselves. Like seeing the young Indian barrister twice in Kyoto to the point that it almost seemed spiritual and some sort of cosmic attraction did exist between me and the unusual British-Indian woman, who was as intelligent as she was beautiful. She gave Iko and me a business card in the subway. Her vocabulary was intellectual and sensual. None of this seemed real. Traveling so far and only to fight in the Tokyo subway system and the barrister trying not to laugh at us. That feeling I had of being in a Duran Duran music video on MTV.

The eclipse came and in time it had slowed down and so did the people. It was a relaxed day and the students themselves seemed to be moving in slow motion. I was tired because I had stayed up late the night before and my body was limp and numb. The sun was so bright that it was beyond the usual Southern California glare that strafes one's eyes. It was an eclipse for some time and I had somehow prepared for it. For me it was an opportunity to write and Jober was going to be taking pictures.

I had closed my eyes on the bus to rest a little bit. Somewhere along the way home the bus had had an accident. There was a big commotion upon impact. I remembered looking at the bus driver's face. She was as calm as her body was rounded. A woman had flown from the back of the bus forward but was amazingly okay. The slow-motion effect wouldn't leave me at all. The vibe was that of a science fiction movie. A nervous bus driver passed out accident cards to be filled out by witnesses. The driver of the other car was an African-American lady. A few passengers floated the common idea of having a sore neck. I filled out the witness card. The bulbous driver smiled and I existed the bus at Martin Luther King Jr. Boulevard. I ate a small mushroom and I walked a little bit to another bus stop. The eclipse was soon to come but he could already feel it. I wanted to get home as soon as possible. It had been a long strange day. My mind was filled with thoughts. I couldn't absorb any more. There was a shade of gray that seemed to envelope everything. Smiles seemed longer than usual and colors were brighter. My imagination was let loose. Los Angeles it seems I had seen it from every street angle. There were eerie mornings when it was quiet and a little bit cold and children were on their way to school and on their parents on their way to work. Walking past the projects and I see a young man swing a baseball bat and break the window of a van. A woman's voice could be heard crying in the distance and I had taken a slow calculated glance but I continued to walk to toward the intended school. It was hard to walk away without wanting to get involved sometimes as apathetic as it seemed, it was better to keep on going. I would deal with it later. Where were the police, I thought. This should not be happening. Now there was the eclipse waiting and teaching became stranger and stranger. The open-target status and the sense that one was doing what was right and for the right reasons. Still there are times when I could not make any changes, it just became hopeless. The bus came and it took me to Vermont Avenue. There was the normal talk and the regular nonchalant behavior. The cowboys and Indians assumed their positions.

There was another dream the night before. This one was softer. I didn't know her but I knew who she was. It was a fantasy and what puzzled me was that it existed somewhere in the back of my mind. We were someplace I never recognized but seemed beyond existence. She touched me and we spoke to each other in a dream language. Her thigh was exposed and maybe she was wearing the lower portion of a bikini. She wanted to take me somewhere but that's where things begin to fade. I woke up sweating. I walked to the bathroom and turned on the cold water from the sink faucet. I stared at himself for a long time and the walls were filled with graffiti. Another rough night of thoughts and she was beautiful I thought. Where was I going? She could have been leading me to my death. Those people were real I thought they existed in their own lives on the other side and stared into the bathroom mirror and reconciled that it was just a dream when in reality he felt something that he knew that he couldn't deny at all. What she wanted from me I didn't know but she was there to take me away. I tried to remember her face. It was Iko. Reality was so harsh and that was what was in front of me. I turned off the lights and tip toed back to my bed. Falling asleep was not so easy as it looked on television. It took a little bit of time. My hair was a little wet. The face of the woman was still fresh in my mind and it would be all day.

Now I was on Vermont waiting for another bus. I was across the street from the Los Angeles Coliseum of USC. It was out of place like a lot of buildings in Los Angeles. The next bus didn't take long to arrive. There's a common theme with bus riding and it was another long, patient bus ride. Sometimes I was too patient. I shut my eyes momentarily, the moon was upon me. The dreams were always presented as if there was a difference between what I could see from the bus window and what I imagined. The lines were blurry and life was sometimes monotonous. Where was the change? Voices became mutated at some point and the women and children who crowded the buses began to resemble hordes of cattle. I battled these hordes every day. People rushed onto the busses only to go the back of the bus, the worst being the phenomenon where passengers would clog the center of the bus afraid to push to the back without utilizing every available space. Each day the archetypes battled each other. Female students put on endless coats of makeup and male students looked for ever-more important ways to flex their masculinity, guilty of acting and becoming characters that they had seen in the movies or on television. There was a certain lifestyle that we all wanted to project and we then became shocked to know that it was all being orchestrated and socially engineered.

My stop was approaching. All the memories and thoughts stopped with each pause of the bus, with each image taken into the mind. Sometimes the only thing you have is a song or a memory of some event. You held onto it desperately milking the feeling for all of its worth before you exhaust it in the face of reality.

Jober awaited. He sat silently in his apartment because work was over and he didn't have to talk anymore or translate any request. Each day he had his own crazy stories about women being beaten or telling a guilty suspect that he would have to do time or where the nearest branch of a bank was and how to find a cousin in a downtown Houston jail. After all of this excitement is time to make music or watch television, answer emails or look at pornography. Still the day was gone was gone and all of his city adventures had become distant memories and pictures scanned to be manipulated on photoshop. I could only dream of having some of those adventures. The stories never seemed to stop and I had my own stories to tell at the end of the day when I would reach Jober's apartment, which had the same number as the apartment that he had lived in, where I live now.

Now I was at Third and Vermont. Jober's apartment was blocks away. The hardest part was trying to get inside the building. The manager was supposedly gay, nosey and complicating. He tried his best to be polite but not without the bit of wit which he used so effectively to get his point across. Being nice was okay but you couldn't be too nice. Sometimes the manager would be standing there and waiting oblivious to me, as I tried to open the glass doors to the well-manicured apartment building. It was always a test and the last resort would be going into the side alley and yelling up to the fourth floor where Jober lived. He would then yell back giving the okay and I would wait for him to come down and let me in despite the obstinance of the smiling manager who gleefully made things difficult and whose friendliness did not make up for his subtle deception.

It was his usual greeting when we met hands except when it seems something exceptional had been achieved like securing some hard to find marijuana now that our primary connection had disappeared and where he could be we often speculated about because it was sudden and mysterious and had put a huge crunch into a part of our existence. Everything's seemed to be timed and soon Jober would be gone too and that would be just as rhythmic as the eclipse that we had both agreed to watch. Jober had witnessed many eclipses from Cali, Colombia. Today it would be the eclipse that could damage the eyes and sometimes I thought that my vision had been damaged by an eclipse I had seen when I was young, even though I was prepared to view it through the pinhole of a box and gaze at its reflection, I thought that maybe that was the reason that my vision had deteriorated and as much as I wanted to see the eclipse I was afraid again that the same could happen again pushing me further towards blindness. It was too early to tell but Jober was well prepared and informed and had as usual done his homework so that he knew exactly what had to be done to view the eclipse and was prepared to take pictures and document them like so many things in his life.

"Look through the small hole of a piece of paper but not for long!" he self-assuredly said to me.

"Alright!" I answered but not without reserve.

"I want to take pictures of the eclipse," said Jober.

"I need to go home and change clothes," I said. I was tired and eager to get home. We smoked a joint together and then I got my things and left to go home. There was a tension that was mounting and soon it would be revealed but now it was time to enjoy the moment. I told him about the bus accident. Though last week we had an argument on mushrooms and passed out on the grass at a park but not before seeing a turtle with tape on its back in a pond at the base of a statue.

PART IV

CHAPTER 13
Colombia

Arrival

When I thought about Mariana I imagined her sitting in the middle of a giant map of Colombia. The edges of the map burning a little bit at a time. It was a country under siege. How could there be so much turmoil and beauty co-existing side by side? I wanted to scream. The flight was long but there were few people on board the airplane. The women seemed to get better looking the further south I went. I felt the tropical heat when we landed in Miami for a layover. A certain fear came over me. My family was scared. I had to get away. Cali seemed like the perfect place to go. I was leaving a fucked up situation but somehow I felt upbeat.

I looked out the window of the airplane as we flew over the Amazon Rain Forest. The green canopy could swallow us up and nobody would be able to reach us for days. I quickly grabbed my stuff after landing and headed out of the airport. Time seemed to freeze. I could hear insects as I entered a sea of faces staring almost expressionless at me as they waited for people to exit the airport. The faces I encountered made me feel like I was walking slowly instead of my usual hurried pace. I was told not to talk to anyone on the airplane or when I landed at the airport. While in customs I met some Columbians who had come from Miami. They were students. They seemed happy to be re-turning home. A small group of Afro-Columbian boys followed me outside the airport and begged me for change. I could feel the moisture in the air. I felt like Martin Sheen in *Apocalypse Now*. My arms floated over their heads as a voice called out to me. It was Gino. I recognized his strange smile as I approached. We shook hands. His friend Eduardo was with him and introduced himself. The young boys disappeared. My hair at the time was long and dreaded and received many stairs from the people. We made it to the car. I was sweating.

We left the airport and drove through what seemed like farmland. It looked poor. We were far from down-town.

"What do you want to do?" asked Eduardo. Gino said he had to go to his girlfriend's house. His daughter was there.

"We can smoke there," said Gino smiling.

We made it to Daniella's apartment. I was surprised at how modern it looked. There was something futuristic about it. Everything looked new. It wasn't what I expected. Daniella was ultracool, slim, shapely. She made your mouth water. She didn't speak English. Eduardo and Gino led the way and we met his daughter who was playing with a doll. Daniella went to an old camera she had on a mantel and opened it and took out some marijuana. She gave it to me to roll a joint. I tried to do it in my own way but she saw that I was having some trouble and took it away from me.

She lit candles and told us to look at them. I stared at them for a long time. The swirling colors and smells enveloped me. They were vibrant and large. There was a staircase that led to a loft on another level of the apartment. Eduardo had already gone up there. I climbed the staircase and saw Eduardo already smoking a joint, blowing the smoke out at small window. He passed the joint to me and I took a puff. It felt good to smoke pot after such a long flight. Everything seemed so cool. After being in so much trouble and finding myself in such scene was quite a contrast. Again it didn't seem real. Gino climbed the staircase and joined us. He had to put his daughter to sleep. Daniella climbed the staircase and then she handed me another joint. It looked perfect. She did it so well. It was too cool. Everything about the place had this aura of coolness. I wondered why Gino and Daniella had so many problems but women like Daniella were rare. She smiled. I didn't know of many girls like Daniella in the States. The women I had met so far were not that exotic. They didn't know how to be. And women who didn't mind smoking weed were a rarity or maybe that smoking out always turned out to be some type of problem.

It was good to smoke there, blowing the smoke out the window. Gino and Eduardo looked happy. Life was moving slowly here but things were happening quickly. I had just landed and things were happening so fast. What to really think of it all? How come the States couldn't be like this?

Everyone descended the staircase to look at the candles. I couldn't stop being amazed at the size and sophistication of the candles. They would sell well in the United States I thought. You could hide drugs inside of them. We listened to music and talked for a few hours but soon we had to move on to Gino's apartment and Eduardo had to go home. Then it was off to the balcony.

"You want to get laid?" asked Eduardo "You want some cocaine? You can go to Cartagena and meet some Italian girls that will suck your dick!"

I smiled and laughed. The funny thing about it all was that he was sort of serious even, though he was joking.

"I'm okay!" I replied.

Eduardo smiled and lit a cigarette. Gino laughed and shook his head. It was hard for him to believe that I was here. Especially after I had been in the United States a year earlier and met him at Jober's apartment. It was hot.

Mariana's House

Everything continued to make me feel as if I was being slowed down. Mariana's face had a troubled look. Somehow she seemed tormented. I should have given her some attention in the short time I was in Cali but I was uninterested or maybe just rudely shy. Our meeting happened too quickly.

She had invited me over for dinner with her family. It didn't seem real. She was so exotic but I felt distant. I had met her a few days before at a party. It wasn't even a party. I was staying at Gino's apartment. They lived well, which had something to do with their class. Their uncle had been killed in downtown Cali. I was a little nervous about the meeting but Carlos, the brother of Gino, who was Jaber's close friend had invited Mariana.

Inside Cali it was business as usual. Everything I sensed was foreign. I had entered the unknown. Mariana looked sad. She was beautiful but troubled, lovely but melancholy. I was so stupid. When beauty stares you in the face and then you run away you feel it, simple things sometimes are the hardest. I couldn't do it all the way that I wanted to. I had to make a fool of myself. Somehow I always did. I really wanted to do a better job of realizing my imagination but somehow I mismanaged my thoughts.

Mariana sitting there in the middle of her apartment working slowly on her computer designing things, that sweet hammock that I fell into like a sugar cube melting on my tongue. She tried her best to let me know but I just couldn't see it, bending over with her ass in my face while looking for something in the refrigerator long enough for me to notice.

How could I be so blind to something so astonishing like a comet that might pass once in a millennium. I would be too old to see something so beautiful again; I didn't know then that I would have to return. If only there was really time to talk. Really enough time to really know what would happen. Women, they know. I was so stupid. I wouldn't put down the camera and talk to her and get to know her. I had taken something for granted. It's in the eyes. When you look, you know. That grin. She was sad but her family was cool. They were Lebanese but I arrived late and didn't have time to eat the dish her mother had prepared. It was basically all gone by the time I had arrived. I don't know why I had made that mistake. I always was in a hurry. Again I hid behind a facade, this time it was a camera.

Departure

Leaving was hard. I had been up all night drinking cases of Poker beer with Gino and his friends. It was our last night together and we wanted to celebrate. Suddenly I fell sick. I remember Gino standing over me near the toilette in his bathroom and saying not to forget about the taxi that would be coming to get me in 3 hours. I lay there on the bathroom floor, motionless, feeling like I would die. At some point I got up and gathered my stuff and made it downstairs to the taxi.

At the airport it was worse. I vomited in the bathroom. Then when it was time for me to get through customs, the officials were suspicious and called over menacing security guards. They asked if I was a mula — a drug transporter — carrying cocaine in my system, inside my stomach. I waved my hands and denied it but that wasn't enough. They called over some vicious German Shepard dogs, started shouting at me in Spanish and cocked their guns and I almost shit on myself. I was terrified and I had to vomit again and I did. To make matters worse Jober had asked me to bring back a porno magazine that basically translated to hand job in English and his sister wanted me to bring back some bras from Colombia because she felt they were better than American bras. The officials were looking at all of this stuff in my suitcase and they looked at each other and they let me go, maybe because they thought I was some sort of horrible pervert. I gathered my stuff. Shut my suit case. I sat down on a chair. Turing around, I got up and I went to the window overlooking the tarmac and I threw up all over it. Waiting passengers grimaced and asked if I was ok and urged me to get some coffee. I felt like a cockroach — maybe Kafkaesque. It was depressing. I thought about the beautiful Lebanese Marianna, lying in her hammock, in her living room and how I kind of let her down for being late to dinner at her house but the Baklava was good and it reminded me of her —sweet. When I asked her father about Lebanon he rolled his eyes and motioned me to eat dinner. I felt good and that I had at least made it to Colombia but this is not the ending I wanted. I thought about Owen, the dread from Brooklyn that saved me from a crack head with pliers in his hands, who jumped out at me in downtown Cali. Owen's family had sent him to Cali because he was getting into too much trouble in New York City. My friends were gracious but the airport was a disaster. I boarded my flight and fell asleep. I didn't remember transferring in Miami. When I finally got to California and landed at LAX, my sister said take a shower because you smell like shit.

CHAPTER 14

I woke up sweating. It was different this time. In my dream, my tooth had disappeared. That fear that I had of being disfigured. It was also the realization that I had been selfish. That I could have done more. I didn't really give as much as I should have. I had all of the regrets, regrets that she said she didn't want to have. Still, I had my dreams that drifted from one thought to the next. There were too many to count. Iko floated in all of them. I had all of the scenarios worked out now. Now I was living a different life. I thought at some point I would run into her and I thought about what I would say. I thought about how she would react. I thought that about how I would say how it was a good thing that we had broken up when we did because we were still young enough to explore life, how it was bad timing, that we could meet in Central Park one day and act like it had never happened.

That last meeting in my apartment on Alvarado was the end. You could just tell by the way everything played out. It felt like slow motion. It was a drop of sweat moving on my skin. I could replay it again and again. It bordered on the edge of fantasy. Something was happening that I was unaware of, always hallucinating. The more that was hidden, the more I knew that something wasn't right. I couldn't always put all the pieces together. That drew me in more. I didn't have the acumen to live life so responsibly. I was worried about things too much. She had finally gotten her wish and wandered away from me. She had disappeared deep into New York. We were closer when she was in Japan and now that she had bypassed me, she was further away. I realized now that I had screwed up. That I had been too selfish, I had no compassion for her needs but she was a social climber. That wasn't my nature. My dreams were about her but unrealistic. That's why I would stay home and just do nothing but read. I might go for a walk and try to clear my head. That time was always there I thought. That first time and that first flight. The return was always the hardest. It was hard leaving, it really was. I wondered sometimes how I did it. I was too attached to her. My dreams that I had in the middle of the night. I could let go of those sometimes but other times I couldn't. It was easier to live in those dreams. It felt better there. I didn't want to come home. I didn't want to come back. I didn't want to wake up. I wanted to stay in those thoughts and that era. I had a crazy imagination but I wasn't living the life I wanted to. I thought about that last night I was with her a lot. I wondered if I had taken too many mushrooms. How I thought that she could have been wearing a costume?

"Costume?" she slightly uttered. I thought I heard those words come from her mouth.

She stared at me oddly and changed out of office clothes she had bought but it looked like a high school girl's uniform. She put on a blue strapless bra with matching panties, bowed mockingly and came toward me and bent down on her knees and looked me in the eye, feeling my penis. My pants were off because I had been watching her undress the whole time. She had arranged panties and bras that she had bought at the outlet mall on the floor in neat rows. She put her hands one the inside of my thighs and moved them toward my penis again. She separated from me at the mall and walked away with her friend. I found them later. Her friend patiently waiting outside of the lingerie shop and Iko inside taking her time. Her friend Kimiko smiled and said Iko was inside and pointed to her in some aisle in the distance holding up a blue bra.

CHAPTER 15

Ivan had disappeared. Mrs. Veracruz was crying through the phone. After all she had done for him and now he was lost somewhere in downtown Los Angeles. Her reservations about arranging for him to live in a low-rent hotel off of Seventh Street, downtown Los Angeles had come true.

What can a mother do with a son who just can't seem to get his life together? It was rough leaving Cuba. The soldiers coming in the middle of the night to hasten her family's evacuation. The fear! A soldier had used the butt of his rifle to hit her. She was eight months pregnant. This was not socialism; it was the end of an empire. Who wouldn't be scared? Now to live such a humble life and to be amongst those with so much more. She loved her present husband event though he had beat her and his children wanted to kill her. That even though he was an artist himself, and foremost a Chicano. He knew fame and poverty and education. He worked with the youth and the criminals and the politicians. He was a zoot suiter and political activist and he knew that everything had a good and a bad side. It was hard for me to be neutral because to take sides would create schisms but Mr. Veracruz read me and all of my education was at times no match for the street smarts of Mr. Veracruz. But having had a lavish lifestyle, Mrs. Veracruz knew that opulence wasn't the answer to life; as an artist she was an educator and Ivan was a little off but he wasn't developmentally disabled.

Life had made him implode. He was extremely emotional and always getting into trouble. He had previously been in jail as an alleged accessory to robbery of a McDonald's. Actually he was taking drugs with his neighbors in his building, when they convinced him to go rob the McDonald's with them. He was booked downtown at the Twin Towers Correctional Facility. People who are incarcerated at Twin Towers die. Paris Hilton was there. It's a bad place. Ivan was afraid and said something to the sheriffs that they didn't like and they beat him with their batons. He was hospitalized for a month. I went to see him. Mrs. Veracruz was calm but inside was hysterical. We found parking which was a miracle and then walked over to the day room. There we had to put our things into a temporary locker which cost a dollar. We were given a number. The place was alive with activity. Some of the families looked familiar to us and some of them were indescribable. Time was the equaling factor. Waiting for your number to be called and then to get up and walk toward the door, and through a metal detector. Then down a long corridor that looked like the entrance way to where some war criminals might have made their last stand in the twentieth century. The elevator took us up and then into a room where there was plexiglass speaking booths. It was familiar because my father had been in jail and I had gone to visit him, and when I left, I placed my hand on the glass to match my father's hand and walked away. This was justice? Everything had been turned upside down like a Diana Ross song.

Ivan had a beard. He seemed motionless and puffy. His mother picked up the phone and talked to him in Spanish. He smiled when he could but he looked like they had kicked his ass yesterday. Mrs. Veracruz was crying. She was going to get a lawyer. She was going to complain. We had gone to the courthouse later and met a lawyer. It was grueling and raining and then there were more problems and things got complicated.

"¿Como estas?" I asked.

Ivan smiled.

He didn't answer. I thought that though he had been beaten down he had made it through the worst part and would be okay. It was fucked up. It sucked when you didn't have money sometimes when it really counted. What could you really do? Still that was not what life was about when everyone was telling you that it is. I was there to confide in and I was her supreme confidant. It was sad. Though she didn't want him to live downtown she was not about to let Ivan go to Miami where his other brothers were living. You make money in New York and you retire in Miami, Florida or California. Mrs. Veracruz was determined to take care of her son.

"Children are for life!" she said to me complaining.

That was something that I wouldn't understand until later now I was consumed by the brutality that is before me. What had really happened? Mrs. Veracruz came up with the documents. She wrote to Sheriff Baca. In between there was Cuban food at El Co Mau or El Conchonito.

"I have an attorney," she would say in between her eating. She had Russian table manners which she had learned when she was young. I just hoped that I was placing my knife and fork in the right place but maybe I was which is why she had told me about how good my etiquette was. I was a good writer and now that I taught, I'm still writing long after I had graduated from college.

"Did you see how they had beat him?" said Mrs. Veracruz. "Did you see his eyes they were swollen?!"

"They beat him those animals! They beat my son!"

I was silent.

All I could do was give Ivan hope and Mrs. Veracruz my advice and opinions. Ivan looked like a political prisoner with his full-grown beard. He looked like someone who was an extreme alcoholic but instead of booze he had been beaten down by sheriffs' deputies in the Twin Towers jail where things are segregated by race and gangs in an overcrowded county jail in downtown Los Angeles.

Here was Ivan, who had traveled out Highway 10 heading toward Arizona. Mrs. Veracruz thinks he took too much acid. That he may have met Native Americans and taken peyote and now was in such a state from all of his psychedelic mistakes and problems and situations in some sort of fourth dimension of time and space. When he was level he enjoyed good conversation and humor. You started to wonder what happened but then it was like he hadn't completely made the transition through all of the turmoil that had disrupted his life and turned him into the person that he had become. He was distorted. I thought of myself and how I was not that far away from where Ivan stood mentally. That he himself had gone over the edge. That he existed in his own emotional state that had done him harm and created so much confusion in his own life.

He had blocked it out for his own well-being in order to exist. In some strange sort of way helping Mrs. Veracruz helped me with my own life. To somehow assist another artist was a release and helped me with my own problem-solving skills.

I couldn't believe that Ivan had been lost. Mrs. Veracruz had made some missing persons' notices that she wanted to post up around the neighborhood where Ivan lived. I parked her white Plymouth sunbird on the sidewalk next to Ivan's apartment building. It was a hot day. The type of day in Los Angeles when I would rather be at the beach than be so deeply involved in Mrs. Veracruz's life but we were somehow cosmologically linked because we both had birthdays on August 29th. The apartment building was on a hill that gradually rose toward Third Street where a giant modern new high school was built that looked like a giant playground for adults. New gentrifying apartments were adjacent to the high school. Third Street was changing. It was so different in the past. It still had its character but how long would it last. Mrs. Veracruz had made the missing persons' signs and then brought them to Kinkos and made copies. Mrs. Veracruz gave me some tape.

"Are you alright?" I asked Mrs. Veracruz

"Yeah, I'm okay, Ivan," said Mrs. Veracruz. Her words trailed off softly.

I looked at her for a long time. She seemed to be in suspended animation.

"Look, I'll take the left side of the street and you can take the right side and then we can meet up at Third Street," I said totally confused.

What else could we do? I kissed her on the cheek. Mrs.

Veracruz crossed the street. Her glasses tinted in the sunlight. She was about five foot six. Her hair was dyed somewhat blonde. She had a large nose, almost like mine but hers was more prominent. I stood on the edge of the sidewalk and watched Mrs. Veracruz cross the street. We each had a reem of tape in our hands. When I saw Mrs. Veracruz go to the first lamppost then she turned and started walking up the sidewalk. I came to the first pole and ripped off a piece of tape and then fastened the white piece of paper onto the pole. It looked sort of strange but stranger was the fact that I had never done this before. The only other people that had disappeared in his life were my mother, which was very brief and my sister, which lasted longer, about a year. It didn't seem like the way they described it in a movie or even on the news. Would anyone even call the numbers listed on the paper? It was a chance that had to be taken. People did it for their pets and I thought that was going a bit far but this was a human being. Someone I knew. Someone I had known for a while even if it wasn't that long, it was someone that was an integral part of my relationship with Mrs. Veracruz which involved her art work, conversation, and her son Ivan, who as long as I knew him had been in some kind of trouble. I could see some of myself in Ivan. That if I hadn't gotten myself somewhat together I could be like Ivan drifting through life. We are artists. That's what scared me the most. That I was as close to Ivan emotionally that I would care to admit. Except, somehow I had gotten myself together. I helped Mrs. Verazruz because I felt it was the right thing to do and that Mrs. Veracruz would help me if I really needed it and she had been there for me emotionally, especially when I thought about Iko and how much her leaving me had left a giant hole in my heart.

Another pole. I glanced across the street I could see Mrs. Veracruz slowly making her way up the hill. Third Street was getting closer and closer. I watched Mrs. Veracruz 1 post up another sign on a pole. Then I did the same. I put enough tape so that the sign wouldn't be blown away or ripped off easily. Finally I reached Third Street. I graduated not far from this area. I remembered how different it was then. I stared at the new high school. It looked like it could fall over. It was futuristic looking. The kind of place that was supposed to inspire students. I put up another missing person paper on a pole at a crosswalk. Ivan looked happy in the picture on the sign. It was a good picture of him. I could see Mrs. Veracruz crossing the street. Last we had to go to his room. We had been there before to help clean it up but this time, it was for good. Ivan couldn't be left alone anymore. His room looked like a rats' nest. Ivan had been cleaner before but something must of troubled him to send him off into the deep end of his mind. We all wondered what was happening inside of the mind of his. That brilliant mind. He could paint too. Mrs. Veracruz had shown me some of his paintings. They were similar to his mother's, abstract, maybe even awkward. It was art, and then what happened?

"How do you feel?" asked Mrs. Veracruz looking at me.

"I'm a little thirsty but I think we should cover the bottom intersection," I said wiping sweat from my forehead.

"I have some waters in my car. Let me put up one more sign then we can walk back down together."

Mrs. Veracruz put up one more sign. Then Mrs. Veracruz and I waited for the light to change and then we started heading south. The sun was starting to go down. "I hope Ivan is okay," Mrs. Veracruz muttered to herself.

The worried look on her face made me want to cry but I didn't want to make the situation any sadder than it was.

"It will be alright," I said. "We'll find him."

"I just hope he is okay," said Mrs. Veracruz. She started to cry.

I hugged her and we stood there on the corner. Cars came by and people stared at us through their car windows but we didn't care.

Mrs. Veracruz pushed me away and then took off her glasses and wiped her eyes.

"I'll be alright. Let's put up some more signs and then I'll leave one in the lobby of his apartment building," said Mrs. Veracruz.

We both continued to walk. Mrs. Veracruz gained her composure. Soon we were at the bottom of the hill. It was Wilshire Boulevard. This end of Wilshire was so different than the hustle and bustle of its western end. I posted another sign. Mrs. Veracruz crossed the street and posted another sign. I followed her and then we made our way back to Ivan's apartment building. The building was old and run down. It sort of smelled and looked deserted but was filled with people. This was old Los Angeles. Mrs. Veracruz asked one resident if he spoke Spanish, then she asked him if he knew where the manager lived. The man said that the manager lived down the hall in apartment number one. Mrs. Veracruz thanked the man and gave him a flyer. Then she headed towards the manager's apartment. She knocked on the black screened security door. She knocked several more times but nobody answered but when the both turned around the manager was approaching and introduced himself to them.

"Can I help you?" he asked us.

"Hello, I'm Mrs. Veracruz. My son Ivan lived here and he's missing," she said with urgency.

"Ivan?" the man asked somewhat puzzled.

"Yes, his name is Ivan and he lives in apartment 209," said Mrs. Veracruz.

"Oh yes, Ivan. I know Ivan. A very nice guy. I'm sorry to hear that. I haven't seen him since yesterday. He looked fine," said the man trying to be helpful.

"He looked alright?" asked Mrs. Veracruz.

"Yeah, I didn't notice anything wrong with him. He looked fine to me," said the man again.

"I wonder what happened?" asked Mrs. Veracruz. "This is my friend Bernal. He's a writer he's helping me try to find Ivan."

Mrs. Veracruz always introduced me as a writer. It sort of caught me off guard but at the same time I liked the fact that she took me seriously as an artist.

The man shook my hand.

Mrs. Veracruz gave the man a flyer with Ivan's photo and contact information on it. The man took the flyers and looked at it for several seconds.

"Thank you for your help. Please call the phone number on the paper if you have any questions."

The manager said that he would contact us right away if he had any new information.

I said thank you to the man and then me and Mrs. Veracruz made our way towards the entrance of the apartment building. The sun was still bright. The lobby of the building was dark. I felt better being outside and away from the smells of the old apartment building.

"Let's eat some Mexican food. I know a place nearby," said Mrs. Veracruz.

We both walked back to her car and got inside it. The car was hot and we both rolled down the windows. She started the car and we had both buckled our seat belts at the same time. She drove to the end of the block and turned right on Wilshire. The restaurant was located on the corner across the street from a hospital. Mrs. Veracruz parked on the corner. We entered the restaurant from the side and stood near the entrance and waited to be seated by a waitress. The inside of the building was airy. The ceiling was high. There were a lot of customers. Mrs. Veracruz and I sat next to a window. Mrs. Veracruz left right away to wash her hands like she always did. While she was gone the waitress came but I told her that we needed a little bit more time. After Mrs. Veracruz returned from the bathroom, I walked to the bathroom to wash my hands. It was a ritual. When I returned we ordered food. Mrs. Veracruz's mind was occupied but I tried not to make her worry.

"I'm so tired. I just hope we can find Ivan. Do you think we should post up some more?" asked Mrs. Veracruz.

"We covered all of the major intersections and you called the police and we posted notices inside his apartment building and told the manager. I think we've done as much as we can. Didn't you call any television news stations?" I asked.

"I called the Spanish station," said Mrs. Veracruz. I also contacted *La Opinion.*

Mrs. Veracruz would always pause.

It seemed like the day wouldn't end. Ivan had disappeared. You never think it's possible until it happens.

Then there was her life as an artist and then there was her relationship with her husband who was also an artist that she complained about because of his verbal and physical abuse but she loved him. I listened to it all because in all that I heard were lessons about life and especially about relationships. The waitress returned to order. Mrs. Veracruz ordered in Spanish. Then I made my order in Spanish.

"Thank you, Bernal," said Mrs. Veracruz.

"It's okay," I said.

"I know this is a lot for you. I know that you are trying to be patient," said Mrs. Veracruz wondering if I had had enough.

"Don't worry about it. I know you would do the same for me. You've been there for me so many times," I said trying to reassure her.

"You still think about Iko?" said Mrs. Veracruz smiling a little bit.

I didn't think such a subject would cheer her up.

"Now you are going to make me sad," I said joking.

"I didn't mean to bring that up. I should have known better," she said smiling again.

I smiled a little bit. Even though she had hit a nerve she could help but laugh at it all. How obsessed I had been. Now it all seemed so funny thought at times it had been so serious that it occupied so much of my thoughts.

"Are you all right?" asked Mrs. Veracruz. "I didn't mean to say that?"

"I'm okay. I thought you were the person who was supposed to be sad?" I asked jokingly.

Mrs. Veracruz laughed. She was still sad but it did help to have some humor.

The waitress returned with my chile relleno and Mrs. Veracruz's tamales. The food looked good despite the somber occasion. I ate my food slowly. I just wanted to take my time. Mrs. Veracruz focused on her food. She took tiny bites and chewed her food slowly. She ordered a beer. I had water. The sun was shining again outside even though it was the evening. Mexican ranchero music was playing then it was suddenly interrupted by a band and a man began singing corridos in Spanish. The music was soft but I thought it was a bit corny. The restaurant was quiet. This guy was supposed to be locally famous.

Mrs. Veracruz turned to watch. I kept eating my food. The sounds from the keyboard resounded off the walls of the restaurant. It was upbeat. Maybe that's what we needed. Posting up the missing persons signs was intense. It almost seemed hopeless but only the strangeness of it all made it seem hopeful.

"I don't really like this music," said Mrs. Veracruz.

I was a little surprised because I thought that maybe she was into the music.

"I thought you liked the music?" I asked.

"Are you kidding! But he has a nice voice," Mrs. Veracruz said smiling.

I wondered if she would ever be satisfied and whether Ivan would ever be found. I looked out the window and the sky was turning darker. The music continued to blare. I wanted to eat my food while it was hot. Mrs. Veracruz had turned around to continue eating her food in little mouthfuls.

"Do you like the food?" asked Mrs. Veracruz.

I nodded my head. I was chewing on some cheese. The food took away both of our problems for the time. It was a nice escape. We could be worrying somewhere. Mrs. Veracruz's beer was halfway finished. She had been pouring her beer in a glass filled with ice. The scene looked tempting but I didn't want to drink. I thought about where Ivan could be. Where would I go? If I went downtown or stayed on the streets for too long anything could happen. I looked out the window onto Wilshire.

A week had gone by. Mrs. Veracruz had called me to keep me updated on Ivan but he hadn't been found. I had just woken up. Last night I had another dream this time about being thrown out of a car. The driver looked like Nora. I was then rolling onto a lawn at a corner house. Then I got up and saw a woman with blonde hair on a horse who came and told me to get on the horse. It looked like Susan. She wore a tunic. She took me on a ride to a house. When we arrived at the house the woman had morphed looking like Iko and she brought me into the kitchen and made me something to eat and then I woke up. Now Mrs. Veracruz had called again because she started to worry about Ivan.

"Hello," I said. I was lying on my mattress in my apartment. I didn't' have a bed frame.

"Bernal, how are you?" Mrs. Veracruz asked.

"I'm okay," I said. "Have you found Ivan?"

"No, we haven't found him yet. I just hope that he is alive. I don't know what I would do if anything happened to him," said Mrs. Veracruz.

"We'll find him, Mrs. Veracruz. I don't know how to make you not worry but well find him," I said trying to reassure her.

"Thank you for coming over yesterday."

"Don't worry about it," I said. "Thanks for the books."

Mrs. Veracruz had given me a book about Santeria. She tried to teach me a little bit about it each time we met. Some of it was sinking in but some of it was complicated. Then there was the initiation. She had given me some beads before and prepared them in a special ritual that involved soaking them in coconut milk. Then she blessed them and gave them to me who put the beads around my neck. The necklace had green and black beads representing the Orisha Ogun. This all had happened yesterday.

"Do you like your beads?" Mrs. Veracruz asked.

"I'm looking at them right now," I answered, lying on my mattress with my shirt off. The necklace was long and I had doubled it so that it would fit around my neck. I had been attracted to the colors but this was no ordinary necklace.

"Read the book," said Mrs. Veracruz. "I've told you many things but you have to read some more on your own." Said Mrs. Veracruz.

I wondered what I had gotten myself into. I fiddled with the green and black beads of the necklace and held the phone in my other hand.

"Hello," said Mrs. Veracruz through the phone.

"Yeah, I'm here," I said.

"Enjoy your necklace," said Mrs. Veracruz.

Mrs. Veracruz was sitting down at her desk. She was staring out the window. She was burning some incense. A picture she had painted of a cathedral in Cuba hung on the wall. It looked ghostly but captured Mrs. Sandoval's childlike artwork that many people admired. More paintings rested on the wall next to the television set. It seemed like a lot of artwork but there was more because I had moved them one day with my truck.

***

Mrs. Veracruz had found her son. He was in the parking lot of a hospital downtown. She was relieved but bewildered at the same time. She had called me in the morning. I was a little bit startled because I had had another strange dream.

"Are you okay?" she asked. I should have been the one asking her that question but maybe because she had been through so much she could not deal with it all so calmly.

"They found Ivan," she said a second time.

"I'm so glad you found him," I said. What could I really say?

"I don't know what I'm going to do. He can't live in that place anymore but I don't know where else he can live. He's in a hospital Do you want to see him?"

"I'll come over, let me get ready," I said.

"You don't sound to good," she said again.

"Did you have another bad dream?" she asked curiously.

"This one was more strange than bad," I said, trying to wake up.

"It's her! I know the sex was good but let it go, Bernal! It's destroying you!" she said in Spanish. "Let me get ready," said Mrs. Veracruz. "Okay! You can come with me to see my son!" she said and hanging up the phone.

I lay back down in my bed. I stared up at the ceiling. I was happy she called and that she had found her son. Things couldn't be stranger. How did all this happen? At least they found him alive, I thought. That poor woman, her son had given her so much grief but at the same time she loved him with all of her heart as only a mother could. It was hard to think that her son was also an artist. I thought back to when I first met him. I wasn't sure what to make of him. He wasn't developmentally disabled. Like me, he had a lot of severe emotional problems and I thought that I could be like him but I had navigated through life in a way where I had learned to not to destroy myself emotionally, but who was I to judge Mrs. Veracruz's son.

Ivan was just crazy. I thought about him again. Our first encounter and how he appeared almost catatonic. What had happened to him? The police had found him in a parking lot. Mrs. Veracruz had gone to the local Spanish television station and told them about her missing son a few days ago. Someone had seen the story on television and reported seeing a man sleeping in a parking lot. The television station called the police and then and then they contacted Mrs. Veracruz and she met the police at the hospital parking lot.

I put on a T-shirt and some jeans, brushed my teeth and left my apartment. The sun was shining bright outside. It hurt my eyes. It made me feel guilty. That maybe I had been inside too long or maybe it was just the strange dream with the two girls on the horses and then the bizarre ending of it all with the food and the refrigerator. It still weighed heavily on my mind and now they had found my best friend's son in a downtown hospital parking lot.

I found my truck and got inside. A man was coming down the street pushing a shopping cart. I thought that maybe he had seen him before but maybe he just needed to wake up. There was a vacant lot across from where I parked and where people tossed trash. A week ago a dead body was found in the vacant lot but nobody would talk to the police and so they just took it away. Now it was like it never happened.

I started my car and headed for Mrs. Veracruz's house. I was happy they had found Ivan. It was the ending to a long chapter. Now the painful part of trying to find a new place for him to live and how to provide some type of treatment or how social services would begin. For Mrs. Veracruz it was just one of many beginnings for her and her son.

CHAPTER 16

I sat on my bed and thought about the beads in my hands and about how Ivan had disappeared and returned. My life was on pause. I thought about Mishima and about the movie *Patriotism* I had seen with Iko before she disappeared from my life. I had a dream about it. Iko was beautiful. I had put a flower in her hair and she had cried during the film. *Patriotism* had only been shown publicly once in America. I looked over at Iko's face. She was focused intently on the film. A tear lay at the edge of her eye.

It was dark.

The setting was formal. I felt a little bit underdressed. There was going to be a discussion afterward. The event was sponsored by the Japan Society of America. Most of them were scholars and businessmen. It was intellectual. The film lasted about forty-five minutes. I gripped the edge of my chair. Everything was dramatic, especially Mishima in his military uniform committing Japanese ritual suicide.

It seemed like a long time had gone by. The room and the movie silence. It was an awkward venue. It was literary and cinematic at the same time. We had spotted an ad in the *Los Angeles Weekly* about the film. It was a limited engagement. It wouldn't be shown again for who knows how long. This was before YouTube. Iko had cut the ad out of the paper and brought it to my attention. I spent a lot of time in her dorm room reading cinema critiques about Fellini's films and the importance of neo-realism. Iko had taken a few photos of me for her photography class, while I read books in her living room. I felt comfortable there. I didn't want that moment to change. There in her dormitory where we made love and ate spaghetti Japanese style and read and fought and dreamed about going to Cuba. She supported my literary passion giving me books by Lafcadio Hern and a watch with Yasunari Kawabata face. She was tall with features that some thought looked gargoylish but it reminded me of a Japanese traditional mask. Her large oval eyes that looked almost cartoonish. There was something about her awkward nose and oval face and wide mouth. It struck me as very mystical. Iko was ambitious, cunning, physical and mysterious. I wanted her all the time but we couldn't marry and she wanted to go to New York.

"I found this in the paper," she said with a smile.

"What's that?" I asked but I hadn't heard her the first time.

Iko stood looking at me for a while before she answered me. She was tall for a Japanese woman. Those long legs which she like to show off with miniskirts and flared jeans. Just enough to keep me interested and everyone else. It was too much for me to ignore.

"The movie *Patriotism* by Mishima Yukio!" she repeated again. But this time I had heard her more clearly and I got up and walked toward her and she handed it to me. I took the paper in my hands and looked at it for a while. It caught me off guard. How prophetic it was because in a weird way it sort of symbolized our relationship. We were running out of time. She would only be in the US for a year and then what? Nothing seemed real anymore. Everything counted. To Iko I appeared to be moving too slowly. I wasn't young anymore and neither was she, and though she was only twenty-one, time had caught up with her. I with my youthful feathers and somewhat slanted eyes seemed untouched by time. I was forever young.

"It's tomorrow night," she said smiling.

I looked up and moved closer to her and kissed her on the lips. Her face lit up, the way it always did when she was happy, but she could easily make the same expression on her face when being cunning and dangerous. I was too naïve to notice. Iko understood something about men and I was learning that I understood little about women. I pulled away from her for a minute.

"I want to go, let's go!" I said smiling again. Iko liked it when I was happy.

"Let's eat," she uttered, excited about tomorrow night.

She told me to sit down at the table. I put the article down on the side, so that it wouldn't get any grease on it from the pasta she always liked to make. She seemed to be always making that pasta. In the skillet that was somehow appeared attached to her robotic-looking arm next to her miniskirt. Boiling some pasta and then after draining it in the sink putting some in a skillet and frying it with olive oil and maybe some butter and then adding some pepper and salt afterward. Then it was served as hot and tasty as can be. The Japanese who seem to use mayonnaise in the weirdest way but it had caught on for me. I started to like it. After serving me she sat down after having given herself a serving. She was so measured. I always seemed to need more and more love than she could supply. Afterward she would say, "That's enough!" like a mother who didn't want her child to get fat from eating too much food. We sat in silence for a while. There was always the gulf between us even though we were intimate as any couple could have been. She had been sexual with me in ways she had never been with any other man but I always seemed to want more and more. One time as a joke she wrote for the whole month of October in my planner, sex in every square for every day of the week and at the bottom where someone could write a note, she wrote, "More sex!"

Iko, who was always mocking me in some way to put herself above me. I tried in vain to unravel her like a Zen koan. There was a samurai part of her and it was true that she was supposed to be from a samurai bloodline which might explain her haughtiness and demanding mannerism. She had studied calligraphy and could draw Japanese characters well and had demonstrated it one time at a party surprising everyone and even me who wasn't aware that she possessed such talent.

"The movie starts at eight thirty," she uttered breaking the silence.

I looked up at her. She was chewing on some pasta and smiling. I smiled back. There was a moment of clarity between us. At least she had found something that gave us some common ground. Mishima had been such a big part of my understanding of Japan. The eroticism of Mishima's writing had captivated me but it was the literary detail that was erotic as well as the bizarre subject matter that had nurtured my romantic perceptions of Japan.

I put my hand on her leg and moved it up her thigh as she continued to eat until she couldn't stand my hand being under her skirt and pushed it away.

"Finish your food!" she said.

I obeyed her like I would my mother. She smiled again as my hand retreated as she pulled a single noble of pasta between her lips and I watched it move in slow motion between her lips and her large mouth and rows of teeth with silver crowns in the back. She said there were only three types of people in Japan. That she was bored there and wanted to get away. I thought she had it all figured out but maybe I was wrong but I also felt that she was running away from something and now that included me.

Dreams...

It seemed like the movie would never begin but when it did it was quiet. Now after some time had passed, after Mishima committed seppuku, the celluloid in black and white, Mishima on his knees and his wife next to him, and the theater seemed more like a wake, with its frigid audience. I looked over at Iko's face. She was transfixed on the film with a small gleam of light on her cheeks, a silhouette of Mishima's wife and to my right, I could see that man in the business suit, looking at the movie screen. He had smiled at Iko in the lobby and she smiled back at him. I turned back toward the movie. There was no music. It brought us to the breaking point.

When the film ended and the lights came on, I looked to my right at the business man and then looked to my left at Iko who was teary eyed and had somehow gripped my hand during the last few moments of the film when the soldier had taken his own life in the dark of his bedroom and now that the lights were on and returning to normal and the audience stirred again like the tide, she slowly released my hand. After the film was over there was a question-and-answer session for people in the audience. The Facilitator was from UC Berkeley, an expert on Japanese literature. I was one of the first to raise my hand and ask a question.

"Why had this film been banned for so many years?" I asked. It was an obvious question, the type of question the facilitator expected to hear and one he could easily answer. A few people in the audience had turned their heads to see who had asked the question. I looked straight ahead.

The facilitator took a few moments to answer before going into some academic diatribe that didn't seem to satisfy me but I already knew the answer to his question but just felt compelled to break free from the silence all around me. Silence that was weighing me down and I knew that Iko would not ask anything even though I had inspired her to learn more about Mishima herself besides the other books which she consumed and I couldn't understand because they were all in Japanese and she never made an effort to talk to me about them. Always never revealing who she really was or what her motives really were until the last minute or never.

I had fallen back to asleep in my apartment I could feel the mushrooms starting to kick in.

I started to dream I was inside of a speeding car. It was the same dream I had before but now I was hallucinating on mushrooms. I was passing through some suburban neighborhood. Large houses with huge lawns. Who was living in these homes? It could have been some place in Pasadena, I wasn't sure. All of a sudden something or someone had pushed me out of the speeding car. I was catapulted out of the car and summersaulted on to a large green lawn. The crazy thing about it was that I could see it happening to me from afar. It was from another angle as if I was filming the whole thing for me to see or someone else was. Then once again I was given another angle. I lay there on the lawn wondering how I had gotten to this strange neighborhood again. The house was on the corner. A large tree was planted in the middle of the lawn but the lawn extended at a sort of obtuse angel around the curve of the street. The grass was very bright. It looked like someone had spent millions of dollars on Miracle Grow. It was picture perfect immaculate. The whole neighborhood looked perfect. I was horrified and baffled by the whole scene. No one was on the street. I stood up. I was wearing jeans and a T-shirt. The mysterious car that had jettisoned me moments ago had vanished. I glanced at the rear window of the car and I could see that it was Nora driving. I had totally forgotten about it after collecting myself from being pushed from the car onto the strange lawn.

The house was large. You could describe it as a mansion of some sorts. The roof was gray and the walls at the bottom were brick and the wooden top part was painted beige. Small shrubbery surrounded it. For some reason I couldn't see the front of the house. I couldn't see the front door at all. I didn't try to move from this position at all. I was somehow stuck there on the lawn. The sun was shining overhead. Where were all of the people?

I heard something in the distance. I couldn't tell where

it was coming from but I knew it was coming closer. It sounded like a galloping horse. The sound came closer and closer to me. I looked around as much as I could in all directions to try and detect where the horse or horses might be coming from. It seemed like the animals should be right upon me but I could not see them in any direction. I turned my head once more to try and get a bearing on what or who was approaching. I thought about Angela, Pauline, Shonna and Lisa but my memory was fading.

I turned again once more only to find a white horse with a strange rider peering down at me. The horse seemed like a giant or maybe it was the breed. Its rider was a woman. I recognized her from a similar dream before. It was Susan. Her blonde hair, with the green streak but it was changing to a darker color. She was not solid but somewhat murky. Another horse was to her side with another rider with the same color hair. Maybe it was Hada or Angela. None of them said anything. One rider didn't say anything but only gestured for me to get onto the horse. It seemed impossible but in some twisted way I was able to mount the horse. The woman set the horse in motion. I put my arms around her waist and the horse began to gallop and take the two of us in some unknown direction. The house and the strange neighborhood faded into the distance. It ceased to matter anymore. The other horse and rider followed behind us.

This whole fantastic universe was beginning to melt. Once again I was transported into another void inside of a house. Sitting at a kitchen table and the woman on the horse, who must have been the rider but she seemed to take on a more definite shape. I thought that I might have recognized her. That maybe she was someone I possibly knew. Maybe from my university but I wasn't sure but she put me at ease and I felt comfortable around her. I wasn't scared anymore. I wanted her.

"Would you like something to eat?" she asked politely in Japanese. I could make out a large Ikea steak knife in her right hand. It had a blue plastic handle. She was wearing a white T-shirt a miniskirt and tennis shoes. She was very relaxed. I was in a kitchen sitting down at a table with my hands in my head but when she asked me if I would like some food, I looked over toward her again. She was standing next to a large refrigerator and held it open a little bit waiting patiently for me to make a decision.

"I don't know," I said in German.

I wanted to know more about her but I was unable to ask the questions that would possibly reveal her identity to me. She smiled and continued to wait, looking a little bit like Iko. I remained at the table and the woman remained at the refrigerator waiting for me to tell her what I would like to eat. There were chopsticks on the table and a picture of woman at the Santa Monica Pier smiling. It looked like someone I knew. It looked like her. My mouth wouldn't move for me to ask the questions I really wanted to ask her. She continued to smile. Her hair slowly changing to black and shoulder length and I could do nothing but look at her and wonder where I was and how she and I had gotten there and why she had picked me up —and why we had galloped through what seemed like space and time until we reached some kitchen—in some house where we could not move and where I was being asked what I would like to eat and then everything started melting and I told her I loved her.

ABOUT ATMOSPHERE PRESS

Atmosphere Press is an independent, full-service publisher for excellent books in all genres and for all audiences. Learn more about what we do at atmospherepress.com.

We encourage you to check out some of Atmosphere's latest releases, which are available at Amazon.com and via order from your local bookstore:

Olive, a novel by Barbara Braendlein

Itsuki, a novel by Zach MacDonald

A Surprising Measure of Subliminal Sadness, short stories by Sue Powers

Saint Lazarus Day, short stories by R. Conrad Speer

My Father's Eyes, a novel by Michael Osborne

The Lower Canyons, a novel by John Manuel

Shiftless, a novel by Anthony C. Murphy

The Escapist, a novel by Karahn Washington

Gerbert's Book, a novel by Bob Mustin

Tree One, a novel by Fred Caron

Connie Undone, a novel by Kristine Brown

A Cage Called Freedom, a novel by Paul P.S. Berg

Shining in Infinity, a novel by Charles McIntyre

Buildings Without Murders, a novel by Dan Gutstein

ABOUT THE AUTHOR

John W. Horton III is a 47-year-old African-American writer and poet living in Los Angeles, California, currently completing an MA TESOL degree at California State University Dominguez Hills. He most recently lived, worked, and cycled in Japan for 9 years, raising a family and delving into Zen meditation.

In 2018, his poem "Black Friday" was published in the *Tokyo Poetry Journal, Volume 5 —Japan and The Beats* (www.topojo.com). He got started writing as an intern and columnist for *the Los Angeles Weekly*. In 1998, he won second place for best columnist from the California Intercollegiate Press Association, at California State University Los Angeles, writing for the *University Times*.

Mr. Horton likes to explore issues of race/ethnicity, gender/sexuality, class/economics, and politics in his writings because of the intriguing social aspect of how these topics create narratives that intertwine among us all. Reading and storytelling are so important—he thanks all of the libraries, independent book and record stores, movie houses, and English teachers and storytellers he ever had, as well as all of the comic book publishers, for feeding his soul.

His influences are many, but he loves the classics— African, French, German, and Russian writers, including Gogol, Dumas, Fanon, Mann, Chekhov, and Hesse. His love of classic Japanese literature includes Yukio Mishima and Yasunari Kawabata, and classical poets like Basho and Busan. American literature influences range from Chester Himes, Ralph Ellison, and Jack Kerouac to Philip K. Dick and Ray Bradbury. Jazz, hip-hop, and other musical genres and cinema are equally influential, and have proven vital to his creative process. However, his central interest is in how different artists interpret the world and how as human beings we all try to manifest our creative thoughts through art.

CPSIA information can be obtained
at www.ICGtesting.com
Printed in the USA
LVHW010013180820
663425LV00003B/306